.Chapter1

The February wind was
drips, up against Greyho. ... ... terminal
doors, Tony Wilson; a 5/7 feet male about
155 pounds and 50 year of age, wearing a
long tan cashmere coat on top of an v-neck
dark brown sweater, light brown pant; with
specks of white hair on the side of his head,
which wasn't the snow outside, emerge from
a city taxi-cab on the run, to catch the 2:00
P:M. bus to Chicago. With a little help from
the wind that day, pushing him though the
first set of doors, with him stepping down on
a banana peeling, that someone had nicely
drop, with snow and ice up under one of his
boots; he slide though the second set of
doors, a passenger was coming out, he
heard over the station intercom, " The 2:00
P:M bus 872, leaving Detroit to Chicago, is
boarding at gate 10; this is your last call for
Detroit to Chicago, thank you for riding
Greyhound." Tony was still sliding toward
gate 10, pass the   ticket counter, thinking it
was a good thing he had his tickets in his
pocket, on one leg and hollering to other
passengers, "Move out of the way!" the
other passengers stare at him in
astonishment, wondering how a person can,
balance their self on one leg like that. Tony
in-pack with gate 10 doors, tripping up the
two flights of steps into the bus, arriving at
the bus driver feet, with the snow and ice

going up under the bus. With a smile to cover up his embarrassment of a quick entrance, said to the driver, " Is this the bus to Chicago?" The driver gave him an extraordinary look, answer, " Yes, this is the bus to Chicago, you just may it on time," he thought, were did this nut come from. Tony, still on the bus floor, handed the driver his tickets, looked down the aisle for a vacant seat, spotted two unoccupied seats, second to the last roll on the right side of the bus, opposite the rest-room, with two elderly ladies setting three seats up from them, with their shopping bags half in the aisle. He did a side to side motion down the aisle, he look like a figure skater, tripping over the lady shopping bag, when the bus went into a fast reverse, he landed in his designated seat, with one arm in the air and the other one clutching his over-night bag, with a smile on his face, looking around to see if anyone seen him, a lady on the opposite side seen his act, saying , " What the matter son, can,t hold your liquor? started laughing. Tony, unwind himself from his bag, put it up into the luggage rack, looked at the lady with a half smile and sit down in his seat by window, to relax from all that sliding to the bus, tripping over a shopping bag, he looked out at the city, wishing his wife was with him, the bus went down on the freeway, to its next stop. He looked back up front, noticing the two elderly ladies, were he tripped over one of their vinyl shopping bags, the one on the aisle seat was larger than her partner by the window, she had on a big hat with imitation flowers around it in February, like she had just left church, a black coat with fur around the collar, making her head look like a turtle head up out of his shell. The other lady in a red hat and red coat sitting by the window, must have been mistaking for a fire hydrogen off a street corner, , the one on the aisle seat was talking loud another for Tony to hear in back of the bus." My name is Pat, that is short, for Patricia," the lady on the aisle seat utter to her partner, on the window seat, through came into her mind, she should have shorten her body to, ": I am on my way to California were the stars are, maybe they will think that I am a star to." The lady by the window, gave her a glance, , thought, how are they going to think she a star, with that wig on and two strings of hair up under it grasping for air, after the thought had vanish out of her mind, said, " My name, is, Lyn, did I see you walking to the station, when I came in? Pat answer, " No lyn, you have me mix up with some else, I never walk," Lyn looked at her strange,

(2)

thought, she don,t want to own up to her profession. Tony ear drums were running over with their gab, when the bus pull into the Allen Park Michigan station, to load up passengers and luggage, he gaze to the front to see who was getting on the bus, notice, two young couples coming his way to the back seats in back of him, the young man was wearing a Army uniform coat on top of a blue shirt and blue jean, with combat boots on, his mate had on a waist side tan jacket, with tennis shoes on in this weather, they were in a fracas on there way to the seats in back of him, they place their bags by their feet and not in the luggage rack. Tony hear a cling, like bottles hitting together inside their bags. The young lady hollered at her mate, "We spend forty dollars! in cab fare to make it here, to catch this bus leaving Detroit, because you had to find a liquor store, did your mother consider getting her tubes tie, so you could, not come out, your daddy wasted fluid with you." Tony thought to himself, they must have had to catch this bus bad, to spent forty dollars, to make it here to Allen Park, (One of Detroit suburb). The young man, with his eyes rolling from side to side, mutter, " You would have been up set, if I had not stop to load up for the trip to Chicago." She gaze at him, insurgent, utter, " It was plenty in the bags Tim, unless you drunk it all, when I had to stop to use the rest-room, with them long pips of yours, that don,t have a bottom, the holiday are over, unless, it is a holiday every day with you? Tim look at her with a s mile, saying, " You love me no matter what, my mother and father lose, in getting me here, so I could meet you." Gail re-bound her words with," That is my problem, "I do love you, I just wish something had blew in my eyes that day, when I seen you, then I would not have to worry about you or love. you." Tony was wishing to himself, he hope the love-birds would go to sleep, so he could rest his eyes, looked at his watch on 2:30 P:M., thinking, it is to early to rest anyway, started looking back out the window. The couple in back of him had clam down, was talking and laughing now with each other, as one of them pat him on his shoulder, asking him his name, as he turn around and seen it was the young man on the aisle seat in back of him, answer, "My name is Tony Wilson," and turn back around. The bus pull off, heading back to the freeway, on its way to the next station, as he started back gazing back out the bus window at the last of the city streets, thought about his wife, wondering why she was so quiet, with tears coming out of her eyes when he left. He remember when him and his wife was young and met, she was seventeen and I was thirty-two, she had a set of twin boys and a girl, I love her, the kids grew on me and I love them to, not only because they were children of God, but children of the one I love, no natter who the father were, they are God and minds now, I was there father, it was up me to protect them from the grips of the world and pray for them,- girls and boys, soon their were three more add to our clan, two more girls, one boy, make us six all together. We had our up and downs, like all couples, but did,t let the grips of the world, pull us apart, we were like basketball players, she would carry the ball of survival and pass the ball to me, that way, we may it work in the world of survival. In the fall I and the twins, would go from house to house, picking up leaves and bag them up, the same thing in winter, but this time, we would be shoveling snow, while my wife and big girl stay home, watching the other children, the twins was big another now to carry their load. now. In summer, we would get up at 6:00 A:M, deliver new papers before it was time for them to go to school, while my wife drove down the street, to pick us up on the other end, my oldest daughter, watch the other children, before she had to go to school. In the evening, we

(3)

would pick up empty bottle off the streets, or where we could find them, deposit at the end of the week, still giving the twins, time to do their home-work for school, all of us, would go to the outdoor market, Eastern Market, on the week-end, picking up vegetable, off the ground when the farmers left, share them with our neighbors, I appreciated and respect and love the twins, being the men they where before they were men. Finally, I got a good job at General Motor, the survive kit ease up, of carrying that ball, and make a few baskets, hoping some more people can make some baskets of survival, who are in the same boat.. The young man in back of him, tap on his shoulder again, shaking Tony out of his thoughts, utter in a falter voice. " You didn't give me time to introduce our-self, I am Tim and this is my wife Gail, we are on our way back home to Los Angeles, after spending the holiday season up north." Tony glance at him, answer, " I am glad to meet the two of you," turn back around again. An hour later, the two couples had stop talking and was a sleep, Tony eye lids became heavy, started to close, he went into dreamland in his mind, with all his children and wife laughing, playing together, when his dream switch to a more horrifying monument, as he was holding one of his twin son's hand and him holding his brother hand who was in the river, his brother hand slide away from his brother hand who was on the bank, he went down under the water, as Tony pull the other son to safety, with him crying, " I didn't mean to leave you !Dwight, come back, come back!. The sun glow started to desolate its self off the snowy landscape and was slowly going down, when the bus hit a pot-hole, shaking Tony out of his dream and awake, with cold sweat coming off his fore-head from the dream, he took his over-night bag down, went into the rest-room, noticing the couples in back of him still sleep, he re-inter back out of the rest-room, after cleaning up after the night-mare, sit back down in his seat, and looked up front, to see the two elderly ladies with their head together, fast a sleep and they hats, tip to one side, Tony thought what could they have in them bags or couldn,t afford night bags. The sun was not quiet down yet and he thought he seen something craw up out of her bag and went back down in it, unless his eyes were playing tricks on him, he turn in back and seen the love birds, in the same position. He thought about his dream, wishing that the first part of it was true and not the last part, the grips of the world has taking each of my sons and I could not do a thing, because you can,t watch kids all day and night when they are teenagers, or young men, the only thing you can do, is pray.. With one of my twin son out in a hospital on the west coast and know one no were the other one is at, the only way, I and my wife knew were he was at, because the hospital call.. Now one is out in Los Angeles California, at the point of dead with H.I.V. and the other one missing, on narcotic, that was the reason my wife was crying when I left, not because I was leaving, but because the pass over went over our first born. You can send them to school and church, you can rise them right, but the

grips of the world, still get a hold of them and its claws went deep in my twin sons, only thing you can do is trust in the Lord and pray. His mind was still racing with thoughts, and another thought, after another one coming though it, as he shook his head back and forward to his mind thoughts of unwanted debris, but his mind was still not clear, as he thought again,with some tears coming out of his eyes, he try to tell his twins to wait until they went to college, or had a job offer out there, now I am on my way to L.A., to see one, hoping he is still a life when I get there, with the money that I had, this was the only way that I could travel by bus, according to his doctor, there wasn't to much time left, that they had
 (4)
did all possible alternative that they could find, the only thing that we can do, is leave it
up to a higher power then us. It is hard to talk to this generation, because they want it now, but it don,t work like that, in this society ,you have to be patient and roll with the flow or you will be grab up in its net work, or wait for the averages to come your way for what you desire .and do right, for your survival, not wrong. Tears came into the corner of his eyes again, when the bus hit a pot-hole in the road, up under the snow and wave a little waking up some of the passengers, including, Tony, who had dos

off from his thinking, shaking, him out of them and his sleep, bringing him back to reality. The driver announce, " We will be in Chicago in twenty minutes, listening out for your gate call, because Chicago is the drop off point for all bus's leaving west to east, there will be a two hour lay over before your next bus, thank you for riding Greyhound." Tony went back to his thoughts about his twins, leaving at age twenty-one, now one is in the hospital at the point of expiring at the age of twenty-five, why did his brother leave him? when they left together. His thoughts was interrupted again, with Tim and Gail in back of him, talking and getting ready, before the bus pull into the terminal, as it was parking, they were up on their feet with bags ready to go, like race horse's waiting for the gate to open.. The bus came to a stop, Tim headed to the front door holding his over-night bag in one hand and griping Gail hand with the other one, waving through passengers, blocking them, as they were getting up out of their seats, with Gail behind him, heading for the goal of the front door, they look like a couple of foot-ball players, one blocking and the other one making it to the front door goal. The Driver gawk at them, standing by him as he was getting up out of his seat, they were ready to go, when the driver open the bus door. The driver walk off the bus in front, glare at them with suspicion, when they came off the bus, he look down at their bags as they pass him, with a we are innocent smile on their faces, they half ran and half walk into the bus station, Tim look at Gail, hollering, ! hurry up, we only have two hours to find a store and stock up for the trip out West," Gail thought, that man has alcohol, on his brain more then me. The driver looked at them again, as they inter into the station, thinking to himself, what have them two been into while they were on the bus, as the other passengers started unloading. Tony reach up, got his bag out of the luggage rack, thinking Tim and Gail are on their way to the first liquor store, they can find open, looked down on his watch at 8:00 P:M, and glance back up front while he started walking that way, seen the two elderly ladies, with their shopping bags, still in the way, fumbling around, trying to leave the bus and talking at the same time, so he decide to sit back down in a seat close to the front, until they were situated. Pat looked at Lyn and muse, " I will take one end of the station and you take the other end, I forgot to tell you Lyn, you have to make ends meet, so I will not spent up all the money, my dear husband left me; when God took him to a higher place, we are the same kind, bag ladies, (Ha-ha)." Lyn gaze at her with eyes goggling, laugh, saying, that a good ideal Pat, all the peas in the pot are the same, I knew that was you who I seen walking to the station in Detroit." They walked off the bus, still chattering about their plans. Tony, over hear their conservation, thought, you can,t judge the book by its cover, he rise up out of his seat and headed to the front door of the bus, thinking he was glad that they finale decide to leave the bus, so he could get by, he slowly walked down the steps, with the bus driver greeting him with a smile, Saying, " You have a nice trip." Tony looked at him, with a smile said, " Thank you," and walk inside the station doors,

(5)

the driver went back on the bus, to inpect it, to see if anyone left any thing, he walked to the back of the bus, then up toward the front looked down, were the shopping bags ladies was sitting, spot a roach crawling around in it, he hurry up, got in the driver seat, drove off to the station garage hoping they have a exterminator there,. Tony looked at the bus moving out fast, from the bus parking space, wondering what was the bus driver hurry, thought, maybe he had a date.. looking around for a vacant seat and up at the station clock, at 6:10 P:M, thought he don't know which time is right, his wrist-watch or the clock time, he spot a seat across from a lady, holding a baby and breast-feeding it, with two other small children running back and forward around her, then, seen Tim talking

to a fellow outside the station while walking
to the seat, with Tim grabbing Gail hand in a
hurry, intering a city taxi-cab.. Tony,
thought to himself, I hope they make it back
on time, or they will have take that same cab
to Los Angeles, sit down in his seat,
looking around at the people in the station
and then at the small children, still running
around their mother, remind him of his kids,
during the same thing when they were
young. He seen a restaurant, thought should
he get something to eat, but didn't have a
appetite for food or drinks, pull his book out
of his bag, and started to read. The mother
must of got tire, of her kids running around
her shouted, !Sit down! Joe, you and Sam,
the two of you are getting on my nerves,
jumping all around." As one of the kids
bounce up in his seat, accidental, knock the
clothing she had on her, feeding the baby,
revealing half of her breast, at the same time,
Tony looked up from his reading. He
thought, the other two must of did a lot of
pulling on that one, because it look as doe it
need to be replenish again. The mother
holler one more time, !Look what you did
Joe,! Now stay sitting down,." Joe, roll his
eyes, which she didn't see , got up again,
and started looking up under the seats, at the
same time tie his brother shoe laces together,
his mother holler at him for the second time,
"Joe! Get up and sit down like I said, what
are you looking for anyway on the floor?"

Joe answer, " Mom, I lost my play car somewhere,." Just get up, and sit back down in your sit, like I said, be quiet like your brother, I will buy you another one," the mother reply. His brother started wriggling around in his seat utter, " Mom, I have to use the bath-room.." His mother looked at him, , answer, "You will just have to wait until we get on the bus, now be quiet like your brother Joe, and wait, " Sam holler, with frowns in his face, !Mom! I can't hold it that long." Tony thought that she better let him use the rest-room, before she have a paddle by her feet, looked across at her saying, " I will take him to the rest-room Miss, if you don't mind; I also have kids at home, when they have to go, they have to use it, the men rest-room is right in back of me, I will stand outside until he come out." The mother reply, " Thank you, that is kind of you Mr." With a I still don't trust you smile on her face, Sam rise up out of his seat, in a hurry and started to walk,, fell on his face, seaming at his mother, !Mom Joe tire my shoes laces together!" His mother gaze at his brother, with eyes goggling around and he knew what was on her mind, he put an expression of I love you Mom on his face. Tony, grab Sam little hand, started toward the rest-room, saying to him; look like your brother is in a little trouble, Sam smile as he went into the rest-room door, Tony turn his attention to the people in the station and then at the front doors, as he notice a lady, with two giants on each side of her.

(6)

Chapter 2

Coming through them, looking like full backs, for the Detroit Lion,s, in African attiring on, speaking the dialect, the lady was dress in all white on , with a real white fur coat, a pretty black complexion, soothe as silk, to match the white she had on, coming his way and pass him, as she smile, the two men had on blue and dark blue top coats, the two men, eyes saying you better not smile back, he seen them sit down three seats from Joe mother.. Sam decided to come out of the rest-room, a man with a black hat and a red feather in it, and black suit on, with a red tie, black over coat on top of it and a black suit case, looking like Al Chapo the gangster went in after him, Tony ask Sam did he wash his hands, when he heard a loud bang inside the rest-room and a holler, !Who the hell stop up this sink, puting water all over the floor.! Tony, took Sam hand in a hurry, with a quick walk to their seats and said to Sam, on the way, I guess you did wash your hands, Sam ran, jump up in his seat by his mother, almost knocking a box of Kentucky fry chicken on the floor, holler, ! Mom, I am hungry, when are we going to eat? With his brother Joe glancing at him with a smile, saying to himself, he will wait, knowing Mom, Sam kept trying to influence his mother to eat, holler a second time at his mother, !Mom, I am hungry," His mother looked at him with frowns in her face and the baby crying at the same time answer, " This is the last time, that I will tell you to wait until we are on the bus, now be quiet and wait. The man in all black came out of the rest-room, slide again out side the door, with his suit case going up against the station wall and him hitting the floor, hollering,! This is the second time, I have landed on my butt," got up, picking his suit-case up, started walking toward the front door, cursing, Tony, had his hand over his mouth, to keep from laughing, looking over at Sam, who had that, devilish smile on his face. Then, glance over at the African three-some, and the lady sitting in the middle of her two chaperon, who was talking in English now, in a loud voice and patting them on their shoulders saying, " Queen Sheba have all the greatness in the world, now I can head back to Los Angeles, with another contract." With all ears, Tony wonder what she was into,and looked over at Sam, with his mother on her cell-phone, talking to someone. Sam had two larger side marvels in his hand, rolling them around in it, Tony thought were would he get marvels at, in this snow, then looked back at him, to

see what he was going to do with them, one
of the marvels fell out of his hand, started
rolling to the hall were passengers walk in
from the bus, on there way to the front door,
Sam make no attend to go get it, just had
that devilish smile on his face, his mother
still on the pone and did,t hear the marvel. It
kelp on rolling as a blond with beaded hair
and a Russia style pink fur hat on and a short
pink fur coat on that reveal most of her
upper legs and pink boots, that went up to
her knees, she step down on the marvel, her
pink suit- case went up against the wall and
bounce back up under her as she was hitting
the floor, with legs in a v shape, revealing
what was not to be seen unless she was
taking a shower or going to bed, there was
two motor-cyclist, with black leather suits
on and red embroidery on the back, saying
the Patriot, red bandanna on there heads,
with black
caps on top of them, turn around backward,
was about ten feet in front of her, as one
who
have the hot-dog in his moith about to bit
down on it, took a quick glance in back of
him
to see what that noise was, seen what he
was not suppose to see and quickly turn his

(7)

head around, but it was to late as the hot-dog he had bit down on went down his throat when he ran into the station ceiling collar,as his pardner start hitting him on the back to loose it .out of his throat. Tony thought there is another young man, who eyes got him in trouble, as the bible say, if one eye give you problems, take it out and see with the other one. The young lady pull herself up off the floor, picking up her suit-case and wiggle down the aisle, not walking, but wiggling as she went toward the front door,, looking around at the men and, she started wigging more. Her rear end look like two pigs in a sack, knocking up against each other. She pass the two motor-cyclist, who finality got the hot-dog out of his throat and wave as she pass, about twenty feet from the front door, she pass a young couple sitting, the young man, mouth drop open like a draw bridge, his mate was eating a sandwich at the time and shove it in his mouth, saying, " Maybe crewing on that will put your mouth back in its right position ", the lady in pink open the front door, stood there looking around at the men and blew them a kiss , saying good by, with a smile. .The station intercom came on with another departure, " The bus for Omaha Nebraska, 1270, will be boarding at gate 20 in 10 minutes, and thank you for riding Greyhound." Tim and Gail was already in front of the gate, passing the driver their tickets, when Tony arrive, as he

looked in back of him, seen Queen Sheba, with her body guards walking away, with their eyes still focus on him as he smile back at them, thinking to himself, good by fellows, I hope you don,t get bit by a lion, turn, to look back
at the passengers at the departure gates, seen the two little bag ladies making there way through them, with the police hollering ! Stop them two ladies," as they may it up to driver, out of breath, uttering, " Can I and my sister go in behind this gentle-man, we just came from back of the line and started having a asthma attack, we have to sit down, to use our inhalers." .The driver looked at them and they way they were breathing, said, " Go ahead in front of him.". Tony handed the bus driver his ticket, who didn't look to friendly, thought about the two bag ladies saying to himself, they just wanted to get on the bus, in order to get away from that cop who was chasing them,, smart sisters and went on the bus, with Queen Sheba and the other passengers following up into the bus behind him, he seen one aisle seat across from the mother and her three children, the same ones, in front of Gail and Tim, he thought he would rather sit back in the rear with them instead of in the middle of the bus, he walked toward the rear, put his bag up in the rack, sit down, thinking again to himself, look like that I have to ride all the way to L.A. with them, oh well; they are a nice

young couple and I need the company. He look up front to see who else was boarding and seen Queen Sheba, looking like an African Queen, she was sitting in the seat he pass up, across from the mother and her children, she smile at him while he was investigating who was on the bus, seen the bag ladies two seats up from her, also the big fellow with his leg out in the aisle, for some one to trip over, with his coat off and a shining bold head,, Tony thought, that weight he is carrying, must have him hot, in front of the bag ladies,who was talking. Pat said to lyn, " How much did you hustle off of them passengers, I make about a hundred dollars, how about you? Lyn, looked at her, saying " About the same, if that cop, have not infer, we would have may more" they started laughing. Tony sit down in his same seat, in front of Gail and Tim, ,
heard them laughing together, as he thougtht, I gress know one want to sit back here in

(8)

 this bar, or smoke. Tim and Gail was still laughing when Tony sit down, he thought, their love blossom again, after their refill of love potion, he felt someone putting

him on his shoulder, he turn around to see
Tim saying, " Hay Pops, was not that you on
the same bus, we where on coming from
Detroit? You don't talk to much, well Merry
Christmas anyway." Tony turn back around
thinking, where have they been for two
mouths, Christmas was in December, and
gaze up front to see who else was boarding
the bus, he notice a 6 Feet what ever inch,
dress in a black coat, and white shirt, with a
black tie, he inter the bus, pulling his hat off
of his head, so he would not hit the ceiling
of the bus. Tony thought, he must be a
police-officer, the way he is dress and that
hard look on his face, his neck was still bent
back, looking at him as doe he was seeing
the Empire State building in New York city,
he look like the Jolly Green Giant they
advertise on a can of pea's, with another pea
about 4 Feet tall, holding his hand, she must
be his wife, Tony thought, they where still
holding hands sitting down awkward. The
driver inter the bus from outside, after
loading up passengers and stood in front,
announcing his name and the rules of the
bus, like he was an drill instructor in the
Marine Corp, " My name is Mack Turner, I
will be your driver to Omaha, Nebraska,
there will be no alcoholic beverages on
board, or radio's without ear pugs, all
smoking in the rear of the bus, this is an
express bus to Los Angeles, California; with
only stop's for maintenance and food, so sit

back, enjoy your trip." The bus pull off to its designated city's, Tim stir out of his sleep, saying, "Did I hear someone mention alcohol, and went back to sleep. Tony, thought he must have not heard the other part, about no alcohol on the bus, glance down on his wrist-watch at Detroit time and adjusted it to the correct time of 8:10 P:M., he started to doze off to sleep at the wrong time, because Gail and Tim had woke up, started talking again, and indulging in their liquid dinner.. The bus over head lights went out and the night light came on, as a silver object luminous off the bus ceiling, when the Jolly Green Giant rise his arms, to get the stiffness out of them, with his mate arm going up at the same time. Tony gaze, said to himself, I knew he was a police-officer, and she is some kind of fugitive with hand-cuff on each other, he could have put her in his pocket, he thought, After being so inquisitive about other people business, his eyes began to get heavy, because Gail and Tim, had went to sleep, it was quite again, he lean his head up against the bus window, closing his eyes for the night .but Tim and Gail started back talking and he looked down the aisle at Pat, who had that summer hat on, with flowers in it, seen her going into her bag and pull out a sand-wish warp in cellophane, she took it a loose, said to Lyn, " Do you want half of this? Lyn, looked at her and ask , " how long it been in bag? Pat

said, " About a day" .Lyn utter " know
thank you Pat, you get sick by yourself ".
Pat bit down on it and fled something
crawling around in her mouth, and open it
all the way up, seeing a roach on the other
end, jumping up and though up on top of
the big fellow head in front of her, he jump
up, hollering at the driver, ! This lady in
back of me just though up on top of my
head." The driver call back, "I can't stop this
bus, for everything, I am on a tight schedule,
go back to the rest-room and clean yourself
up.".
 The big fellow squeeze out of his seat, grid
his over-night bag, looked at Pat, she smile
 at him saying with her eyes, I am sorry, he
wobble to the rest-room with food on top of

(9)
his head, looking like a salad bar. Tony,
seen him coning his way, thought, he look
like a pot belly stove, they use to burn wood
in, started to laugh, but cover his mouth,
when he seen the big fellow getting to close.
Tim look at him utter," Maybe your hair
will grow
 back and laughed, he just looked at him,
rolling his eyes, went into the rest-room,
About
a half hour later, big man came out of the
rest-room, looked at Tim, who turn his head
toward the window, with his hands over his

mouth to keep from laughing, the big fellow just wobble back down the aisle to his seat, put his bag back up, putting on his cap and over-coat on and squeeze back into his seat, his mate looked at him, with her nose turn up, saying, ""I wish there was another seat some where, that you could sit, in until we get some where, that you can change your clothes." He look back at her with frowns on his face, utter, "I will ask the driver can I go in the luggage carrier when he stop, so I can get my seat-case, pull his cap down on his eye, so he could go to sleep, she put her scars from around her neck and tie it around her nose, did the same thing, went to sleep. Pat rise up out of her seat, Lyn looked over at her, whisper, " Are you headed to the rest-room to clean that bag out, you better hurry up, before we have a ethnic on this bus", she looked at Lyn, roll her eyes, started toward, the rest-room, Tim seen her coming, put a boyish smile on his face to say something and Gail said " You better not say it and mind your own business." Pat went into the rest-room, put her bag on the floor, started shaking out clothes with about five roach,s falling on the floor with her stepping on them, but one got under the door and craw up on the back of Tim seat, she turn the bag inside out and shake it out again, wash the inside out with some paper toilet, pick up the ones off the floor, flesh them down the toilet, put her clothes back in it, walked out the rest-room toward her seat, Tim was about to say something again and Gail gave him that look, he pull his cap down to go to sleep. Pat reach her seat put her bag up this time by Lyn bag and sit down, Lyn looked at her, whispering again, Did you get all of them roach's out of your bag ". She just looked at Lyn, with frown's on her face, pull her hat down and close her eyes for the night. The roach that came out of the rest-room, was on Tim seat, had manger to craw down on Tim neck, Tim jump up hitting his-self around the neck and during some kind of dance, to shake the roach off, Gail looked at him, utter, 'I new it was ,time for the patter wagon with you drinking all that liquor, it has finality got to you? Tony looked at him, said , 'What are you doing, a tap dance for us, before we go to sleep? Tim pull his key ring out of his pocket, that had a little flash light on it, shine it on the floor, spotted the roach, step on it and sit back down in his seat saying "Neither one of you, don't say a word." Tony and Gail, just laugh, closing their eyes for the night The morning sun pierce Tony eye lips, waking him, as he looked around to see who else was awake, rub his eyes from an uncomfortable sleep, thought he better get into the rest-room, before the other passengers wake up. He pull his over-night bag out of the over-head rack, getting his toilet articles out of it, went into the rest-

room, sit down on the toilet, flush it before he got up, a rock came up through it from the road hitting him in the buttock, with a holler he jump up, waking up Tim on the other side of the door, on the
aisle seat by the rest-room, Tim looked and seen Tony was,nt in his seat, shouted

(10)
,

though the rest-room door are you alright in threre Pop,s" Tony answer, " Yes Tim, I just drop my bar of soap and hit my head up aganist the rest-room sink." and smile,.
thinking to himself, that he couldn,t tell him what really happen, Tony anwswer back
rubbing his behind, he was thinking about, why don,t they put a sign up here
don,t flush the toilet while you are occuping it. Tony came out of the rest-room, slowly
sit back down in his seat, with frowns on his face from the ordeal in the res-room, Tim
tap him on his shoulder, mutter, " I know how your back part feel, the same thing happen to me on another bus trip," and laugh, waking up Gail; as she gaze at him with an inquisitive look on her face saying, " What are you laughing about this early in the morning, Waking up people?. Tim, smile at her uttering, " I was just thinking of

something, that happen, in the pass, go back to sleep and get your rest." Gail looked at him, thought to herself, I knew it was time for him to go off the deep end and close her eyes, verging back to sleep. Tony said to himself, I am glad he didn't tell her what happening, that would have been quiet an embarrassment. The driver announce " We will be in Des-Moines Iowa in an hour for your breakfast and bus maintenance, listen out for your gate call and leave your luggage in your seats, because other passengers will be boarding, you have an hour for your breakfast." The bus pull into Des- Moines parking space, came to a stop, with Sergeant Mack, the driver, went out front as the big fellow squeeze out of his seat, put his bag in it with his wife, coming out behind him, he said to her, " You go get a table, order breakfast for us, I have to talk to the driver and see can I get my suit-case from up under the bus," .she reply "All right dealing, don,t be long, we only have an hour " and walked toward the station doors, he said to the driver,." Sir,can I get my suit-case out from under the bottom of the bus, so I can change my clothes.". The driver, looked at him, uttering, " Are you out of your mind, or some kind of nut, if you think that I am going to pull out all of that luggage to find one suit-case, there is a min-mall inside the station, maybe, you can find something in there."He wobble off looking like a penguin, to the gate doors, Sergeant Mack thought, I hope they have something to go around that three hundred ponds. Tim flounder up out of his seat, with what energy he had ,waiting for the other passengers to leave, mutter to Gail, "I guess we have to eat, an hour is not another time to fine a store ", looking like a car just, ran over them, while they were sleep, they pass, Tony as he got up out of his seat, grasp his bag out of the rack, putting it in the seat, looked around and seen he was the last one coming off the bus, Tim and Gail, taking their time to the station back doors, with Sergeant Mack kept looking at them, shakeing his head and thinking, poor kids I hope they can make it to L.A., as they.walk into the station, Tony follow them, with their indisposed eyes and blood shot, he looked at his wrist-watch on 9:35 A:M, thought he better get behind them, a little closer , just in case they don't have another energy to make it were they going,, with him about twenty feet behind them, they went into a restaurant, over to the right side of the station. Tony seen a clothes store next to it, with the big fellow in it, looking around, he went in, hearing Gail hollering, ! Here is a seat Pops! You better hurry,or someone else will get it." He stroll over to were they where and sit down, looking around, met Queen Sheba eyes making advances at him, smiling, waving to come over to her

table, pointing at a vacant chair by her, he
turn his vision to another view as she put a
frown on her face. Tim and, Gail had start
back eating their breakfast with Queen
Sheba looking at him again, winking her
eyes, he order his breakfast from the
waitress, averting her eyes with what ever
she had on her mind, and try not to look at
her, started to talking to Gail and Tim, to
keep from looking at her, winking eyes and,
love gestures with her eye advances. At the
same time, he seen big fellow wife over at a
table by some dinner booths, with Sergeant
Mack, sitting in them and thought how did
he get in here, with me not seeing him, just
like a Marine, always, seeking up on
someone, he was sitting there reading a new
paper, waiting for his breakfast. Tim was
already eating and. jump up and grip his
stomach,, dashing to the rest-room, Gail
look at him walking and half running. Tony
looked, seen the big fellow come, in
wobbling toward his wife table, where she
was setting, turn all around so she could see
his outfit, his wife looked at him,
saying, "That is nice darling, now set down
and eat, we don,t have to much time," he
had his hand on his plate when he started to
sit, all four legs of the chair, gave way,
from the weight,   the plate went up in the

air and Sergeant Mack look up to see what the noise was , but it was to late, the plate land on his Greyhound uniform cap.

He jumped up, throwing his new paper down, walk toward the rest room cursing, big

fellow pull his self up off the floor, the waitress ask him did he want another chair, he looked at her shaking his head saying, " I and my wife will set over there in the booth, they sit down, he look at his wife, uttering, "I have to use the rest-room" and walked off with sad eyes. Tim was in the toilet stall, hear someone cusring and look up under the stall,, seeing a pair of side fifteen boots, thought, that must be the driver, no one else on the bus, has feet like that, he waited to hear the driver leave out and he left out, going back to his table, after sitting their about five minutes, he jump up again, running back to the rest-room, unfastening his pants belt at the same time, with his eyes down to see what he was doing and did not see the big man coming out, the rest-room.and bounce off his stomach, Tim pants went down around his ankle as people looked at him, one man said, " Can,t keep your pants up young man, or is they to big? He pull them up, just another to run to the rest-room toilet stalls, Big fellow did not feel the in-pack, kept on walking. He set down by his wife looking sad,   his wife looked at him, saying " Don,t   feel bad darling, I love you, and care for you, I did not marry you for your body, you are the nicest man I have ever knew, that pretty smile with them dipoles in it and that big heart of yours, helping who you can and me, is the life of our love, I will always be with you, any women would love to be your wife, but I have you, ." put her arms around him as far as they could reach, putting her head on his chest. Everyone in the restaurant clap their hands. Tim came back to his seat, all of them started out of the restaurant and heard over the station intercom, " The bus 1270, for Omaha Nebraska, is now loading at gate 12, have a nice trip and thank you for riding Greyhound." Top sergeant, was at the

front of the gate saying, " All passengers, who was on the bus, load first, so I can get a count, and all others load last." Tony was behind Tim and Gail, as they reach their seats,

taking their over-night bags out of them and sit down, putting them on the bus floor, Tony sit down in his seat, thought, I am glad Top Sergeant did not check anyone bags in

(12)

the seats, or them two would be in trouble, gaze up front to see who was boarding, when the driver inter saying, " I hope all of you enjoy your breakfast, now sit back and relax for

the rest of your trip." Tony thought, he is not all Marine as he pretend to be after all, look at his watch setting on 10:35 A:M., as he fix his eyes back out the bus window, then back up fount, to notice four Golden Girls, with two in the front middle seats and two in back of them in seats , about five seats behind the driver,. They had taking off their hats, and Tony notice that their hair was white as snow, but they were nicely figure at their mature age and appropriate dress in their attiring, as he thought, there sit about three hundred years up front, with the four of them, then he focus his eye's on the other side of the bus, across from them and seen two fellows, with loud color shirt on in this weather, like they had just came from Honolulu, Hawaii with haircuts in the style of trench's going around their heads, to catch water if it rain, with pony tails flapping in the air as they

were talking to each other. On the same side of them, was the Jolly Green giant and his captive, talking in a low key voice, about something that Tony couldn't hear in back. " I

am glad, we seen another police-officer in the station, to take these hand-cuff off of us, and I am sorry that the key was lost playing around," he looked at his wife with sad eyes. She smile with love in her eyes at him, reply, " That is all right honey, you don't have to apology, we had not been this close in twenty-years," putting her head on his shoulder. Tony thought, they are a little to cozy to be cop and robber, started looking back out the bus window at the snow on top of the farms, as they pass them, when bottles started knocking together, like chine's on someone fount poach, when the wind hit them, Tim scream, "All of them are empty! What are we going to do for the rest of the trip." Gail answer with an inconceivable gaze on her face, utter, " Sleep you nut, sleep." Tony thought, I hope Top Sergeant Mack, didn't hear what Tim was screaming about, look like they are out of their love potion, as he was thinking, Sergeant Mack announce, " We will be in Omaha, Nebraska in an hour, you have a two hour lay over, while the bus is being service and change of drivers, also lunch, before your next bus, I hope that all of you enjoy my company and driving and thank you for riding Greyhound." Tim eyes brink wide open awake and said to," Gail did I hear the driver say we had two hours at our next stop?, because his head was spinning with a hang over and his whole body was jittery, as he stare out of the window, waiting for that hour to pass. Tony glance back up fount, seeming that some of the passengers was still a sleep, accept for Queen Sheba, who must of felt him looking that way again and

turn around, smile, winking. He evade her
eyes again, started looking back out of the
window at the snow, after he thought that
she had turn back around, he gaze back up
fount and seen Joe looking around suspicion
for another victim, the mother baby crying
for its breakfast, she put a cover over her
and took out her breast, so no one could see
her breast, pull it, out and started feeding the
baby, with Joe still looking for a victim, to
victimize..The bus pull into Omaha terminal
and came to a stop, with Tim and Gail up
out of their seats, running down the aisle
before
anyone else was out of their seats, Sergeant
Mack, gaze at them standing by him, as he
was getting up out of the driver seat, walked
off the bus, with them on the heels of his f
eet, the three of them walk off the bus,
looking like trebles, Sergeant Mack was still
gazing at them, passing him with a we are
innocent look on their faces, half walking
and half running to the station doors, with
their over-night bags, Top Sergeant kept
staring at

(!3)
them going though the doors, of the station,
thinking to himself, I know them two have
been into something on the bus. Tony was
the last to leave the bus, pass the driver, he

utter with a smile, " Are you having a nice trip, so fare, jar head (Marine), this is his my
last stop, you will have another driver the rest of the trip, you have a good day." Tony started strolling toward the station doors, turn around, looking back at the driver, thinking how did he know that I was in the Marines, I guess one know another one and walk inside the station. He looked up at the clock on the wall of the station, on 12:35 P;M, and thought it is to early to eat again, as he looked around for a seat and out the front doors of the station, seeing Tim talking to another fellow, as before at the last bus stop and grab Gail hand running to a city taxi-cab standing at the front. Tony, seen a seat, sit down to read his book, thinking about Gail and Tim, hoping they make it back on time
again, like they did in Chicago, started back reading, when another thought came into
creation in his mind, about how he miss his wife and children and wishing he was still on
the road to L.A., before it was to late, to see his younger twin son in the hospital, who is only ten minute younger than his missing brother, looked back at the clock on the wall again setting on 1:00 P;M. He heard the mother and her children coming out of the restaurant in back of him, laughing and

talking, with Queen Sheba behind them, she view a seat over next to Tony, sit down looking at him with a captivate expression on her face, recited in her enchanting African accent, " Hi there handsome bird-nest, have anyone claim your nest? If not , I can be your love-bird for the rest of the trip, in your nest." Tony snarl back, with cold eyes reply, "My name isn't bird-nest!, there is a claim on me, my wife is at home waiting for my return." Queen Sheba rise up out her seat, stroll about ten feet away, turn around with a debonair expression on her face, reply in a soft voice, " I will be up a few seats from you on the bus bird-nest, if you change your mind," she strut to another seat on the opposite side of the station, with her back turn toward him. Tony started back reading, rolling his eyes, at her back were she was sitting. The terminal intercom came on with another departure, " The bus 1270 for Denver, Colorado, will be loading at gate 12, in twenty minute, thank you for riding Greyhound." As he gaze up at the clock on the wall, at 2:15 P;M., Tony ramble to gate 12, seeing Tim and Gail running though the front doors of the station out of breath, with Tim running lop-sided, all most dragging his over-night bag, as they reach him in line, still out of breath, Gail utter out of breath, " Hi Pops, are you are you alright?. Tony looked at her, smile, with a reply, " Yes Gail, you two should have been track stars,

the way the two of you came though the
station doors," Gail laugh, but Tim was still
gasping for his breath and couldn't laugh or
talk, as he was bin over with his hand on his
legs, trying to find air to breath, Tony look
at him, said, " Are you alright Tim?" He
mutter," Yes Pops a little out of shape". The
new bus driver was in front of the gate
saying," All passengers, who was on the bus
load first and all other last," Tony was in
fount, of Gail and Tim inter the bus
as they went back to their same seats in back
of the bus, sit down, Tony looked back up
fount, seen a elderly beard gentleman,
handing the driver a city bus transfer, as he
swerve
from side to side, ask the driver, in a not to
sober voice, " Is this the bus to Church
street?" The driver in a nice clam voice
answer, " No Sir, this is Greyhound, not the
city bus." The elderly man walked off the
bus, shaking his head as he wobble back
into the station, saying to himself, that bus
driver just didn't want me on the bus,
because he think that I had a few drinks.
Tony thought that, gentlemen, better be glad
Sergeant Mack
    (14)
 wasn,t in fount of the bus, the new driver
inter the bus annoucing his name, "My name
is
 Bobby Black, I will be your driver to
Denver, Colorado, we will stop at 5:00 pm.

for your dinner, just sit back and enjoy your trip." After the bus resume, we were back onto the highway, Tony thought, that is a switch from Sergeant Mack, the new driver and him must of never met, started looking back out the window again for awhile, then back up fount, meeting Queen Sheba eye's, as she wink at him again, he thought, that woman eye lids are going to lock on her one day if she keep winking at people, switch his eye's over to the opposite side of the bus, were Lyn and Pat was sitting, five seats up from the driver with big man and his wife behind Queen Sheba, his leg out in the aisle, for someone trip over, Queen Sheba, had turn around while he was investigating the other passengers, he
thought she must be asleep. Than focus his eye's at the police officer and his captive, as the rise his arms again without hers, Tony thought he must of free her in the name of love; that will mean, he will have to take her place in a jail cell. His thoughts and visualizing was interrupted with Gail tapping him on his shoulder saying, " Pops, what did you do for two hours in the station? We had a good time, you should of came with us, staying along to much is not good; it make you think about your problems and that is bad." Tony reply, " You are right Gail, how did you get so knowledgeable at your age? Gail shout, , ! At my age!" As she started having hiccups at the same time, she

was trying to talk and said, do you know Pops (Hip), " I am a old lady at twenty-two (Hip) and Tim is a (Hip), old man at twenty-five,". Tony looked at her with a fatherly smile, turn back around, her hiccups was getting more active, Tony ask her did she have a empty paper bag, she said I have plenty of them, Tony advise her to blow in it three times, after each blow, count three times, she started blowing in the bag, Tony, turn back around again.. Tim looked at her, while she was blowing in the bag, saying, " You look just like Alvin and the chip monk, with your jaws all putt out, blowing in that bag, Gail roll her eyes at him and reply back "Go back to sleep (Hip) or what ever you were doing and leave me along (Hip),"Tim, set back up in his seat with blood shot eyes saying,, "Baby,I did not mean to initiate you, but you do," she just look at him while he was talking, kept blowing in the bag, what was on her mind, he would not want to know. Tony was just listening, with a smile on his face, thinking, they are in their mating season, disagreement, they must be out of love portion, I hope that is not the only thing, that is keeping them together, as long, they keep their disagreement at a limit range,of disagreements, they will make it through their mating season, with the love they have for each other, thinking, he wish the clock would go back on him and his wife, Gail mutter, " Thank you Pops, I love you," then took the bag and burst it. The bus sway to the side of the road and stop, the driver went outside to check his tires for a flat, he walk around the

bus looking at each tire, didn't see any flats, re-enter the bus, looking in the rear at Gail, who pretend to be sleep on Tim shoulder. The driver pull back on to the road, thinking to

himself, I wonder what do them passengers in the rear seat be doing, while I am driving and pick up speed to make up for lost time, Tony looked back out of the window, holding his mouth, so no one could hear him laughing about what Gail had did, with her laughing in back of him. Tim stir out of his sleep asking Gail, " What are you and Pops laughing about?" Gail answer, "We were just joking about something, go back to sleep and dream you are at home in L.A," Tim roll his eye's at her, close them again, and went back to

 (15)
Chapter 4

sleep, the driver was looking out of his rear view mirror at them, wishing that this bus was equip with a camera in the rear. Tony gaze back out of his window at the landscape, still full of snow and icicle on the trees, looked back up fount seeing Sam one of the mother kids, playing with a toy bow and arrow, with an suction cup on the end of the arrow, while the mother and other two children was still sleeping. Sam looked around suspicion, Tony thought, someone is going to be in trouble again, Queen Sheba looked across the aisle at him, pointed at Pat hat with the flowers around it, while she was still sleeping, Sam took aim at her hat, miss fire his mark, hitting her in the fore-head were it stay, with her wig landing on the passenger in back of her, starling her out of sleep as she felt her head, which was bald. The man in back of her scream, when he touch the wig, that had felt on his lap, when he touch it while he was sleeping, dreaming about rodents all over his body,. From eating a double Decker ham-burger, before he went to sleep, !

What the hell is this in my lap!, were did it come from? " Sam mother woke up with the

man scream, ask Sam ," what have you been into this time?" With little tears coming out of his eye's and a look of integrity on his face, he utter, " Mom, I thought there was a bee flying around her hat, I didn't want her to get sting." Pat looked at him with a incredulous expression on her face, thought were did he fine a lie like that in his little mind. Queen Sheba was laughing with her hand over her mouth, the mother put her baby in her seat and took Sam, by his hand, leading him toward the rest-room, pass Pat who was still rolling her eye's, with her head, looking like the reflection of the sun off the moon surface, and the arrow still stuck in her Fore-head, she turn around in her seat, , snarl at the man in back of her, ! May I have my belonging back?" The gentleman eye's dilated, when he seen her bald head with the arrow, still stuck in her fore-head, like she had been in an Native American up rising-and got scalp in the battle, his mouth   -

drop open as, he quickly close it, trying not to laugh, he answer, " Here it is Ma'am, I hope that you are alright?" Pat reinstated her wig, and hat back on her head, taking the arrow out of her fore-head, while Lyn was turn toward the window of the bus, with her hand over her mouth laughing, thinking, now there is a Hollywood star as she said, kept on laughing , so Pat couldn't hear her, with Queen Sheba across the aisle during the same thing. Tony heard noises and crying in the rest-room on the opposite side, waking up Tim, as he groan to Gail, " Are we in L.A. Yet.? Gail gawk at him, said, " Nut, go back to sleep, we are along ways from Los Angeles." Sam and his mother return from the rest-room, with him holding his buttock, rubbing it, they started back down the aisle to their seats, passing Pat who eye's was still goggling at Sam, the mother pick her baby back up out of her seat, Sam slowly ease

down in his, when his brother Joe started to laugh, his
mother said, "shut up, or you will be next! Joe mouth shut close, like a clam being attack by an predator, he looked at his brother, with a banter smile on his face, said in a low
voice, " Are you alright, I told you not to be naughty." His brother, just gaze at him, did not say a word, but put frowns in is face, thinking, I will sock you, if you say another word and look across the aisle at Queen Sheba, who just smile at him, saying in a low voice, so that his mother couldn't hear her, " You should listen to your brother and quick being naughty." Sam looked at her in a ire expression, thought, that old witch signify me into getting a whipping, now she is innocent, her time will come before we get off the bus, his brother kelp preaching the do good serenade, until Sam was tire of his mouth,
holler, ! Shut up Joe or I will sock you! His mother looked at him said, " You still have
(15)
not had another of the rest-room?" Sam slouch down in his seat and looked over at Queen Sheba again, who was still smiling at him, utter in a low voice, " I love you to." Sam gaze at her with malice, started to close his eye's for a nap, when his brother Joe was about to say something, put his finger up against his lip, to express don't say

a word. Tony, thought I am glad mom did not hurt that little fellow in the rest-room, I know his butt is sore, it a job, risen kids,when they want to do one thing and you want them to do the right thing, boys and girls, but it is fun, actual. We are rising each other and we have to deal with it, all of us was into some kind of trouble when we were young and when we got older, what can you do but rise them and have fun, and love them, what come around go around, what is going to be, will be so just live and be happy with your children. Pat rose up out of her seat, started toward the rest-room, passing Tim on the

way in, who was awake leering at her hat, utter, before she close the door, " I think that I

seen a hat, like yours in the museum, but it was on a junk horse; you know the one's that

use to go down, the neighbor- hoods picking up junk." Pat eye's ire at him, closing the door of the rest-room, Gail gave him, the same look saying, " Why didn't you stay sleep?" Talking about other people that way and beside that, she is older another to be your mother." Tim put on a childish expression on his face saying, " I am glad she is not," taping Tony on his shoulder, he turn around to see what Tim wanted, looking him in the eye, he utter to avoid his guilt feeling, " Are you alright Pops?" Tony gaze

at him with a fatherly chastising smile, answer, "Yes Tim, but sometime a person. Have to think and notice what they say to another person, before they open their mouth to say anything, so not to hurt their feeling.'' Tim sit back up against his head rest, like a little boy who had been chastise for being bad, Gail looked at him with her big eye's said, " I love you nut, Pops do to." Tim put a wide smile on his face, but drop it off, when he seen Pat coming out of the rest-room, as she was still rolling her eye's at him, when she pass him on her way down the aisle to her seat, sit down, putting her hat in her lap, with a indignant expression on her face, Lyn glance at her, utter, " What is the matter Pat." She leer at her, answer in a melancholy voice, " The bus is getting a little warm," Lyn thought to herself, she still have her coat on, unless she is having middle age hot flash's, looked back out the window. Pat mind was in a daze, thinking that her hat did look attracted on her, close her eye's to take a nap. An hour later, the mother baby started crying, she check her diaper and pick her up, carrying her toward the rest-room
when she went in with the baby, Tim looked at Gail said," You want a baby like that,
Gail just looked at him, the mother came out of the rest-room, fifteen minute later started back down the aisle to her seat unknowing, that she had forgot to unstop the

sink in the rest-room and cut the water off
completely, as little drops of water started
dripping in the sink, with in an half a hour
the sink was full, water started running off
the top of it and down on the floor, through
the door up under Tim boots, as he shouted, !
Where did the Mississippi river come from!
Tim rise up out of his seat, went into the
rest-room, unstopping the sink, cut the
water off, thinking they need a maintenance
crew on this bus and walk out to his seat,
sitting down, Gail looked at him, saying "
You look as doe you are a little wet and
laugh, Tim couldn't say anything, with her
remark, but gaze at her. Tony, rise up out of
his seat to use the rest-room, hoping it was
dry another to use it, , went in, but this time
he didn't intact with the toilet, but squat
above it, when the bus went into a curve on
the highway, catapult him head first into the
rest-room wall, with

(16)

his pants falling around his ankles, he was
holding his head with one hand and trying to
pull his pants up, with the other one. Tim,
call though the rest-room door, " Are you
alright in there Pops?" Tony answer, " Yes
Tim," thought, another embarrassing
movement, as he came out of the rest-room,
with a smile on his face, Tim look at him,
seeing a small bump on his forehead, when
he came out of the rest-room and sit back

down in his seat. Tim pat Tony on his back, muttering, "It look as doe, you have a hard time in the rest-room Pops, maybe you should wait until the bus get to a station to use one,? and laugh, waking up Gail, who ask what was he laughing about, Tim answer, this is between me and Pops, we were joking about something, go back to sleep and rest yourself, Gail roll her eye's at him, then close them again. Tony felt the little bump on his forehead thought, maybe he should take Tim advice and wait until the bus stop to use the rest-room. Queen Sheba, started strutting down toward the rest-room, as Tony quickly re-place his cap back on his head, before she reach him, she smile saying, " What is the matter Bird-nest, your nest is cold, or are you hiding another love-bird up under, that cap and bump on your forehead?" Tony, roll is eye's at her as she went into the rest-room, , thought, how did she know that I had a bump on my forehead, with this cap covering it, unless that woman is psychic. Queen Sheba re-enter from the rest-room, passing Tony and didn't say anything, but stroll to her seat, sitting down, Tony thought she is up to something with that silent and started looking back out the bus window for a while, at the snow and little trace's of sun light coming though the dense clouds, when Gail tap him on the back inquiring, " What are you thinking about, so deep Pop's?" Tony answer, " Not to much of anything Gail, just looking at the scenery, wishing that the time, would past faster, and this long ride is over with." Gail acknowledge, I know, Pop's, it is boring, when Tim interrupted their conversation and said, it is just like the military, hurry up and get ready and go no where fast. Tony laugh, saying " We will be to our destination, when the time is right, for us to arrive, it is kind of like life, you have to wait for each destination you arrive at, that is something that I should rely and relax, for the rest of the trip." Gail looked at Pop's," I no what you mean, the only thing we can do is ride, eat and

go to sleep, until we get to were we are going," lay her head on Tim shoulder, closing

her eye's mutter," That is just what I am going to do, sleep.". Tony focus his vision back up front, looking at Pat and Lyn, who was still gabbing about something, Queen Sheba,

must of felt him staring her way and turn around, again winking , he switch his eye's over toward Sam, who had turn around smiling at Pat in back of him. Lyn gaze at her, uttering

"You must of forgot about your little incident." Pat answer, " No Lyn, kids will be kids," and the two started laughing together. Tony thought with maturity, people can all ways forget and forgive, then another thought inter his mind, that every time he look up front, his eye's mean Queen Sheba eye's, like she had a set in the back of her head. Queen Sheba, glance over at the mother, who head was bobbing up and down, while she was holding the baby, uttering, " You look like you could use a good rest, from the baby and boys, do you want me to hold her or him for a while, so you can get some sleep." The mother, with an falter voice answer, " That is nice of you Miss, she is a girl, I am a little on the tire side," pass the baby to Joe on the aisle seat, who pass the baby over to Queen Sheba, the mother sit back in her seat resting on the head rest, close her eye's. Queen Sheba looked at the baby, like she was one of her children, an hour later, the baby started sucking on her thumb, Queen Sheba gaze at her saying in a nice soft voice, the baby is

(18)

hungry, let me see if there is still some milk in these mature breasts of mind, she put her shawl around the top of her and put one of her breast nipple in the baby mouth, said there you go, if that one don't work, we will try the other one. The mother woke up, out of an dream about someone feeding her baby, looked across the aisle, at Queen Sheba and her

baby and scream, ! What are you doing with my baby!" Queen Sheba looked at her with a impeccable smile, answer " The baby was hungry, so I decided to feed her, while you was resting in peace." She gave Queen Sheba an extraordinary look, quietly said in a low voice, " I think that your breast's have dry up along time ago, and beside that she is my baby, to breast feed." Queen Sheba, gaze at her with an indignant voice mutter, " Young lady, these mature breast's, have brought more children in the world and fed them, than you have age, beside that it felt good with her pulling on these mature breast's again." The mother gaze at Queen Sheba in horror said in an falter voice, " Pass my baby back to me, you sexual proverb!" Queen Sheba pass the baby, back across the aisle to her, with an irk smile, big man in back of her, started laughing, she turn around and ask him, " what is so funny, have you ever try drinking water, for a few mouths, and quit eating everything you see, than maybe that big belly of yours will disappear, I wonder if a pin was stuck in it would you fly all over this bus like a ballon, you look like you are nine mouths pregnant." he just had his arms fold around his chest and did not say anything to her, but look with wide eyed at her, with his mind and eyes doing the cusing, his wife look at Queen Sheba, saying in a lound voice, !You don't talk to my husband like that. Queen Sheba roll her eyes at her replying ,'Be quiet, you little rum, the wife mouth open to say something, but Queen Sheba, close her eye's

for a nap than she said to her husband "Don,t worry dear, we will be in Lincoln soon, away from that crazy lady". Tony, look back up front again at Queen Sheba a sleep, shaking his head, thinking, what have that woman been into, now resting so innocent, with her head bobbing up and down, he turn his focus back out of the window, thinking that he wish his wife and other kids, was with him as he dose off to sleep, a dream pop into his mind, about his wife in the hospital with
 Intravenous needles in her arms, him hilding her hand, saying we will fight this cancer
 together, when another dream came into his mind, about his twins at the river and one
drowning, with him saving the other one. The driver announce, " We will be off the road,
, in Lincoln, Nebraska in twenty minutes for your dinner, you have an hour and a half, before the bus departure." The ones that was sleep eyes pop open and started getting ready, only Tim, was still sleep, The bus came to a stop in the terminal, the driver went outside to the luggage department under the bus to unload the luggage for the passengers that were staying in Lincon.. Big fellow and his wife came up to him, saying " You know that you have a lady on the bus , I belive, have   escape from the nut house ", the driver looked at them, , while he was

still pulling luggage out saying," The whole bus is full of nuts, " went back to work as they pick up their suit-cases and walked away to the station, with the wife uttering, " The driver seen like he is a little on the nut side to. ". Everyone esle started unloading with Gail shaking Tim, awake, telling him it is dinner time, he woke up out of his sleep for a second, looked around to see were he was at, rubbing his eyes from sleep, said, " I don,t want any, you and Pops enjoy yourself." Tony look at Gail and reply, "That hang over is kicking his butt,, he has got to let that liquor along and put some food in him, that would help him, if he eat." Gail said."I will being him a sandwich back". All the passengers for Lincoln, started departing off the bus, with Gail
(19)
and Tony behind them, as they went into the station, seen the restaurant to the left, stroll in, looking around for a table, they seen a vacuum table in the middle and sit down, with Tony noticing pictures of farm machinery all over the walls of the restaurant and others
of large farms pictures, when the waitress came to their table to take their order for
dinner. Tony, gaze over at Gail, who had little tears at the corner of her eye's, utter " Are
you alright Gail, or are you thinking about Tim?" She flagrant answer," You hit it on

the spot Pops, hc is on my mind a lot, it seen like he is trying to make what the doctors have said about that pernicious disease, and its intermittent until the end, he is trying to make it earlier than a year, as the doctors analyze, with all of his drinking, I guess that is the only way he can endure what might be ahead of him, also that is the only way he talk to me, saying lovely word when he is drinking, other then that he is silent. I drink with him, to be his companion and his wife, he need someone by his side, but it is wearing me down Pops, I love him, but he is dragging me along with him, to the grave." Gail lean her head on the table, started crying, Tony put his hand on hers, with a perceive expression on his face, said," Gail some time the doctors make mistakes, they are only human to, it is not up to them, it is in the hands of the Lord, " as he thought, he did not want to tell her, that he was on his way to the same problem, he did not want to add more to hers, he put his hand on her hand again on the table, as the station incom came on, " The bus for Dennver, Co, is loading at gate 8, thank you for riding Greyhound." All the passengers line up, re-interning the bus, to their designated seats, Gail woke up Tim, gave him his sandwich, Tony had started looking back up fount to see who was boarding, notice a John Wayne style cowboy,0 with his head bend down, so he would not hit the ceiling of the bus, with a big ten gallon hat on and a little short partner, with the same kind of hat on, which was to big for his head, because he kelp pulling it up out of his eye's, his other partner, an Mexican following behind them, with a big sombrero on (Mexican hat}, sit down in the seat, two seats in the middle from Queen Sheba. Tony look down on his wrist-watch on 5:35 P.M. Saturday, and thought we are in Nebraska n ow, leaving Detroit on a Friday at 2:00 pm., that not bad for Greyhound, he looked back out the window for a while, than back up fount again, noticing the cop and robber was no longer with us, but Queen Sheba was, still making eye's at him, he turn his sight over to the mother and her kids, who had went to sleep, but Sam,, who was looking around suspicion, holding something in his hand and started down the aisle toward the rest-room, with an devilish smile on his face and had a small play water pistol at his side, so no one could see it, but Tony did, as he pass him, he looked at him, with that same smile and went into the rest-room, Tony thought their go Damien, the little boy character, that play in the motion picture the (Omen, 1976), and said to himself, that young man could use an exorcism. He seen Sam coming back out of the rest-room, starting back down the aisle, with that same smile on his face, to his seat, Tony thought he is up to something, as he seen Sam

looking around for an fresh victim to
torment, while his mother and other kids
was still sleeping, than he turn around in
back of him in the middle seats and spotted
the tall cowboy sleeping, with his hat pull
down over his eye's and shot his water pistol
up on the ceiling above his head, when little
drop of water started dripping down on the
cowboy neck, waking him up with a holler,
!What the hell! Is it raining outside and this
bus is leaking?"He looked at Sam up front
of him who had an innocent expression on
his face, while he slid his water pistol
between him and his brother seats, when he
seen the

(20)

cowboy getting up out of his seat, heading
toward the rest-room, looking back at Sam,
walking in John Wayne style, with his arms
to the side, like he was about to draw on
someone, looked back at Sam with a I know
you did it smile on his face and finish his
stroll to the rest-room. About ten minutes
later the cowboy emerge from the rest-room
and seen three um-occupied seats, right by
the rest-room across from Tony and Tim,
and call down the aisle to his partners, " Big
Jack, you and Poncho come on back to the
rear, here are three um-occupied seats, right
by the rest-room, we can smoke back here,
grab my bag and come on back." Some of
the other passenger's woke up, turning their
head's toward the rear, to see if there was a

loin in back growling, with the coarseness of
the big cowboy loud voice. Tony took a
glance in back of him across the aisle at the
tall cowboy, while he was getting relax in
his new seat, right across from Tim on the
opposite aisle seat and seen him pull out a
big cigar from his pocket, lit it, while he was
waiting for his partners to come down the
aisle to their seats. Tony thought this bus,
will look like the clouds up above Mt
Kilimanjaro in Africa in the rear, with Tim
and them smoking at the same time, I hope
this bus is equip with oxygen masks. The
other two partners, may it down the aisle to
him as the small cowboy ask, " Were do you
want me to put your bag Tiny in the rack or
down by your seat?" The big cowboy
answer, " You can put it by my seat Big
Jack,." Tony heard, the big cowboy calling
the small one Big Jack and thought someone
mix up their name's and side at birth, Big
Jack sit in the bus window seat, Tiny,sit in
the aisle seat across from Tim, as Tony
thought, this is going to be one hell of a trip,
with the Jesse James game across, Tim, and
Gail in back, by the bus rest-room, I hope
that I will make it to LA in one piece. Big
Jack, bent down, reach into his bag, pull
out a bottle of Tequila with some paper cups,
and pour some in a cup saying, " Here
 you go Tiny, that cigar will taste better with
this. Tony took a glance across the aisle at

them, seeing, Big Jack pouring Tequla in the other cups for him and Phoncho as Tiny utter, " You are right, Big Jack , it is better, with a little kick to it." The aroma from the cups of Tequila, woke up Tim, who must have had an hound-dog smell for alcohol and looked across the aisle at Tiny, with big eye's, utter in a soft voice, " Hey cowboy, what are you drinking over there?" Tiny reply, you want some little fellow, if you are man another to take it? Tiny looked at, Big Jack and said, " Pour the little fellow some, and let us see if he is a man." Big Jack, did as Tiny said, pour what was left from his bottle, with the worm in the bottom into a cup for Tim. He turn the cup up, without looking in it, and swallow with something else beside Tequila, going down his throat, his eye's become wide, started rolling around to each side for a few seconds, and once he had pull his faculty back together, looked at Poncho asking, "What was in that drink?" Poncho gaze at him reported, " My young friend, there is always a worm at the bottom of a bottle of Tequila, to give it flavor, you was not suppose to swallow it, but suck on it to get the flavor." Tim grab his mouth and ran into the rest-room, with Gail and Tony laughing with tears coming out of their eye's, Tim re-enter from the rest-room, rubbing his stomach from the strenuous active in the rest-room, sit back down in his seat, with the cowboys laughing and Tony, with Gail doing the same thing, she looked at him still trying not to laugh uttering, " I warn you about, drinking everything you see, other people drink as soon as you hear a bottle open, your nose stick up in the air." Tony was thinking, he needed that laugh, looked back out the bus window for a while, then back up fount to

(21)

meet Queen Sheba eye's again,   looked away from her, over on the opposite side to Sam who was sleeping like an angle; which he was not,   turn his eye's back over to Queen

Sheba side, at the two fellows with pony tails on, still flapping as they talk. The Golden

Gris were during the same thing, talking about what they were going to do, when they get

to L.A., that he couldn't hear in back of the bus." We are going to have a good time out in L.A., with the stars Lucille," Victoria declare, to her partner on the aisle seat, You are right Victoria, answering her and turn around in back of her, said to the other two ladies, what about you Rosie and Jane, don't you two think so? Jane answer with little optimism, " I hope so Lucille." Pat and Lyn were in back of them as Pat mutter to Lyn in a low and soft voice," Them old bags, think they are going to get to the stars, before me, but they have a different thing coming, because I have a plan." Lyn looked at her, with a she need help smile and thought to herself, she must been out on the streets to long and look who is calling another one an old bag, then turn her head back looking out the bus window. Tony focus his eye's back up fount and seen Sam waking up, when he heard the baby crying and started looking around to see, who he could antagonize, but didn't see anyone and went back to sleep, Tony look down at his wrist-watch setting on 7:00 P:M, as the sun was going down and his eye's begin to get drowsy, from the motion of the bus, Tony slip into a nap. A dream enter his mind about his wife in the hospital, with intravenous needles in her.

Chapter 5

Arm and him holding her hand, saying, " We are going to fight this cancer together, when
the other dream about his twin son's inter his mind again, at the river bank, with one of them holding on to his brother, who was in the water and him holding on to his other son, as his brother slide away up under the

water and him pulling the other one to safety, with his brother crying, I didn't mean to leave you Dwight, come back, come back. When he felt someone patting him on his head, waking him out of his dream, he looked up and seen Queen Sheba, smiling at him, saying " Is that a sparrow nest or an Eagle one, do you want a humming bird up there to peck on it to see if anything is up there?" And enter the rest-room, before he could get a word out of his mouth, he holler though the door, !What did you do that for! and don't call me bird-nest any more, that isn't my name." rubbing the top of his head, thinking, he hope she get flash down the toilet with the rest of her waste, Queen Sheba re-inter from the rest-room, smiling at Tony, who was still rolling his eye's, stroll down the aisle, turning back around, look at him with a smile and said," Is handsome bird-nest better." He just looked at her and didn't say anything, but watch her walk to her seat, turning around again, winking at him, Tony turn his is eye's toward Joe, across from her to avert her eye's, as Joe was talking loud to his mother, " Mom, I am hungry!" His mother looked at him saying, " You are all ways hungry, beside that, didn't you just eat a few hours ago, see if there is some chicken left up in the luggage
(22)
rack." Joe reach up there, pull the box of chicken down and looked in it, saying to his

mother, " There is only two pieces left Mom.
". His mother answer, "You should of stay
sleep like your brother Sam, well eat the one
piece , if your brother don't want any."
 Queen Sheba looked at Joe and then at the
chicken leg and said, " Let me see that
chicken leg kid, so I can see if is all right to
eat." She bit down on the chicken leg and
ate most of it, and with an smile on her face
saying to Joe," This chicken is not fit, for a
King or Queen." Joe mouth drop open like
his bottom jaw went into lock jaw, after he
receive his chicken leg back from Queen
Sheba, half bone and half chicken and
scream to his mother, ! Mom that lady ate
my chicken!" The mother looked in
astonishment at Queen Sheba and holler, !
What did you eat my son chicken for?"
Queen Sheba answer in a persuade voice, "
Would you rather for him to be sick, from
eating bad poultry, or me?" With a smile on
her face, still chewing the chicken, what was
left of it in her mouth and close her eye's for
a nap. The mother mouth was still hung
open like someone had put a dentist chip on
it to hold it open, Tony looked up fount and
seen Queen Sheba head bobbing up and
down, like a chicken pecking corn off the
ground, while she was sleeping and she
suddenly holler out,"!Who in the hell put me
in this chicken yard, with all of those
chicken!" She then looked around and seen
the other passengers gawking at her, hoping

that she was not about to fall off the deep in, of her mind. Queen Sheba put on a I am okay smile on her face and rise up out her seat, strolling toward the rest-room, thinking to herself, she shouldn't of eaten that little boy chicken, pass Tony licking her tongue out at him as she went inside the door. He wonder while he was shaking his head, do she have all of her mind facilty and what else is she going to get into the rest of this trip, and thought her and Sam must be partners in crime on this bus, when she came back out of the rest-room, while he was still thinking lick her tongue back at him, for the second time on her way to her seat. Tony just looked at her, when the driver announce, "

We will be in North Platte, Nebraska, in about an hour, there will only be an half hour lay over, to load and unload passengers, you can get off the bus and stretch your legs or stay on the bus." Queen Sheba, turn around in her seat smile at Tony, then lick her tongue out at him again, and at the mother across the aisle from her to, Tony just turn his eyes back out of the bus window and thought, that lady is insane. The bus pull into North Platte terminal and came to a stop, Tim ask Gail, did she want to stay on the bus or get off and look around, because he had to find a rest-room better than the one on the bus, Gail answer "No Tim, I will stay on the bus, with Pop,s until you come back. Tim started down the the aisle, toward the fount door, turn around saying" Are you show, that you don,t want to use the rest-room in the station?and laugh Gail look at Pop,s and said "what are you going to do about that lady up front, who keep smiling and making eye advance,s at you? Tony utter, "I don,t know, she is just lonely and want a companion, but I can,t be it, L.A is still a long way off, I hope someone will broad the bus, who will me her need,s so she can quit winking at me".Gail started joking with him saying, "What the matter Pop,s, she not hot another for you," and laugh. Tony just look at her and smile. Gail then ask Pop,s " What did Tim mean by that remark, going to the rest-room? he shook his head, saying he didn't know, and thinking about Tim big mouth about his rest-room experience on the bus and glad he didn't tell Gail them. She watch him from the bus window coming back, said to Tony," I have to see where he is going sometime, because he get mix up on his direction." Tony, turn around, smile at her saying," I know

(23)

Gail, the war does um-usual things to people." Tim return back on the bus, with a relief on his face from using the station rest-room, saying to Tony, " You should have join me Pop's, it is more comfortable then

the bus," and laugh again, then looked at Gail, utter "
I feel better honey ", who was gazing at him, wondering why he keep laughing at Pop's,
Tony kept hoping he would keep his mouth close and gave him a look of shut up about the rest-room, Tony was rolling his eye's on the other side of his seat, thinking, I hope he close his big mouth, I wish I knew were a clip was at to put on it and, hope Tim don't let the cat out of the bag and go to sleep.. Tim tap Tony on the shoulder, ask him, " Hay Pops, were you in the military? I was in Nam, that is short for Vietnam, pick up some kind of disease they call agent orange, but I will be alright, as long as Gail is with me and that so call medicine work, with my own kind of medicine, they couldn't kill me over there, so they put me on a waiting list here, but that is alright, I get a hundred percent disability from the Government." With some tears at the corner of his eye's, Gail interrupted him saying," Don't start that again Tim, I am with you." Tony answer Tim question about the military, after him and Gail was though pampering each other, It took Tony, a minute " Yes Tim, I was in the Marine Corp in Korea along time ago, I am sorry to heard about your mishap, but we may it home, were a lot of us didn't, I only came out with a little scraper in my right leg and still limp around, but I get were I am going." Tim holler out, !

I knew you was in the service, the way you walked and talked!" Tony looked at him with an fatherly smile reply, " Don't worry Tim, the Government will take care of
 us wree ever we are at," turn back around in his seat from talking to Tim. Tony gaze
back up fount again, to see what new passengers was boarding the bus, seeing two young couples strolling with hands together, like he was about to loose her, as Tony notice a bulge pulling the young lady plain black coat she had on, buttons apart and the young
man with a gray coat on open, with over hall up under it, like he had just left the farm. The young man seen two seats in fount of Queen Sheba and let his mate in by the window and he sit in the aisle seat, Tony gaze at the young man, who was on the nerves side, while he kept looking at his mate stomach, he thought that young mother to be, have sit in the wrong seat, by Queen Sheba, started looking back out of the bus window, at a full moon shining down on the snow, making it look like crystals on the ground, with small and large animal foot prints in the snow, from the reflection of the moon, an Over-cast went across it, taking away the beauty of winter, as he looked down on his watch, setting on 10:00 P:M., then at Queen Sheba, rising up out of her seat, heading his way toward the rest-room. She pass him with that same smile, tap him

on his shoulder saying, " Hi there bird-nest," and close the rest-room door, Tim tap him on the shoulder, utter " Pops, that lady have a love note for you." Tony turn around in his seat, looked at Tim, with a irk smile and mutter, " Well I don't have one for her," still rolling his eyes, as she came out of the rest-room and started back down the aisle to her seat, turn around saying to Tony, " I will be up in that nest of yours yet," sit down in her seat, after molesting Tony, she look at the young lady in fount of her by the window seat, who had her hand up rubbing her hair, Queen Sheba notice her wedding rings , said, " How are you two love birds, I see that you have just been marry, with them beautiful new wedding rings on." The young lady, with a proud look on her face, twiddling her finger with the rings on it reply, " Yes Ma'am, they are pretty, we got marry this morning in Platte, we are, on our way back home to Ogallala, Nebraska." Queen Sheba, eyes brink back and forward

(24)

utter,, " Were is that? Is it that highway light I see coming up down the road?" The young lady laugh, answer," No Ma it is about three hours ride from here we couldn't drive, because of the weather and my condition." Queen Sheba rise up a little out of seat,
 looked at her stomach, smile, saying in a nice quiet voice, "I see what you mean about

your condition honey," the husband was listen to Queen Sheba, thinking to himself, did we sit in the wrong seats, next to this lady? Ten minute later, the young lady looked at her husband with a smile, utter, " I have to use the rest-room dear," she slowly rise up out her seat, while he waited in the aisle, took her hand, because of the motion of the bus, leading her toward the rest-room, with her saying quietly as they waddle down the aisle, what nut house, did that lady in back of us, brake out of, her husband reply, " I was thinking the same thing dear," as she went into the rest-room, shaking her head. He lean up against Tiny seat, for balance, waiting for his wife to return from the rest-room, Tiny looked at him, muse, " You look like a father to be? I think you could use a drink to calm your nerves," pour him some Tequila in his cup and handed it to him saying," How soon will it be," Drink up young cowboy, you are going to need it, before the baby arrive." The young man looked into the cup, said, " What is it?" Tiny utter in a quiet voice, " It is Tequila, my young cowboy, to put hair on your chest and pull the man up out of you," he put the cup up to his nose and smell the contents, drink it, his eyes look like two stars about to have a supernova, said to Tiny, " Wow! That had a kick to it." Tiny just smile,

Chapter 6

when his wife came out of the rest-room,
grasp her husband hand, with the two of
them
waddle back down the aisle to their seats,
she looked into her husband eyes saying, "
Are you sleepy dear?" His eyes was still half
sparkling, when they sit down in their seats.
Queen Sheba, tap the young lady on her
shoulder saying, " Are you alright dear?
Your husband look like he could use a
stimulant, or already had one." The young
lady looked at husband, who turn his head,
so she couldn't see the childish expression
on his face, she just gaze at him, rolling her
eyes and didn't say a word, close her eyes
for a nap. Tony seen Sam coming his way to
the rest-room, with that same demon smile
on his face, holding something in his hand,
walking pass him and went into the rest-
room. Tony thought, someone is going to be
in trouble again, Sam re-enter from the rest-
room, holding something dripping in his
hand, at his side, Tony looked at him in the
half darkness of the bus, while he may it,
back to his seat, his mother and brother with
the baby, was still sleep. The young mother,
woke up saying to her husband, " Dear, I
have to use the rest-room again," he wipe
his eyes from sleep, took her hand, helping
her to walk toward the rest-room, when she
went into the rest-room out of sight, Tiny

hand her husband, another cup of Tequila, with a smile.. He smile back at him, turning the cup up to his mouth, without a word, drink the contents, as his body went into the same chain reaction, like after his first drink of Tequila. His wife came out of the rest-room, looked into his eyes saying, " What is happening back here, when I am using the rest-room," he focus at her and glib, " Darling, you are in a little stress, because the baby is near, we just talk while you are in the rest-room, now let us go to our seats, so you can get off of your feet," she smile at him, with love in her eyes, took his hand, as they stroll down the aisle to their seats. Tiny tap Big Jack, uttering, " That young man, know how to manipulate his

(25)

woman, to keep out of trouble, what is that word Big Jack?" I think you are trying to express soothe talker, the two started laughing together, waking up Poncho, who pull his sombrero up out of his eyes, mutter, "What are you two laughing about?" Tiny answer, " The young man, has became to the age of maturity, with a few drinks of Tequila in him," the three started back laughing. Before the couple reach their seats, Sam was looking
around, with a balloon fill with water in it, Queen Sheba pointed to the mother seat, Sam

smile at her and reach across the aisle, putting the balloon in the young mother seat, the
couples didn't see him reach over to her seat, because they were love talking and looking at each other coming down the aisle. The husband let his wife inter into her seat first, then he sit down on his aisle seat, she slowly sit down on top of the balloon, in her seat, a funny expression came on her face and muse to her husband," Honey, I think the baby is coming, my water have just broken." Queen Sheba and Sam had their hands covering their mouths, so no one could hear them laughing, the husband jump up out of his seat, like his water had broken, hollering at the bus driver, ! My wife is having a baby! Pull over." The driver pulled over on the side fast, knocking some over-night bags out of there luggage racks, with one landing on top of Tiny ten gallon cowboy hat, with him hollering, " That did it!, Put me off at the next stop," Big Jack and Poncho was laughing so hard, that tears was coming out of their eyes, with Tim on the other side of the aisle, bend over in his seat, laughing to, Gail just gaze at them, shaking her head, thinking, all of them have lost their minds.. The driver got up out of his seat, after pulling over to the side, asking was there a doctor on board, a little elderly man, behind Lyn and Pat answer,

"Yes driver, I might can be of help," reaching down by his feet, picking up a black bag,
that look like the same age as him, he proceeded down the aisle to the young mother and said with a father smile," Now let old Dr. Wallace, see what your problem is?" Her husband shouted, ! Her problem is, she having a baby!" Dr. just glance at him, didn't say a word, but proceeded by reaching in his bag, pulling out an instrument, that resemble a piano toner, put his stethoscope to her stomach, then to his ears, after that examination, while her husband was still gazing at him, Dr. said, " Now open your mouth wide, for old Dr. Wallace, so I can see where the problem is." The husband mouth drop open, his eyes became wide, like an owl and shouted, ! The baby, is not. Coming out her mouth! And, what kind of doctor are you any way?" After the doctor, had finish examining her, utter, " You are alright my dear, it is not time for the baby at this moment, but soon," turn his eyes with an indignity gaze at her husband, declare, " I am Dr. Wallace, a license Veterinary and is known all over the west young man, if you need me again, which will be soon, just call, if that is all right with you,." the husband, look at the doctor, " I hope not, for a animal doctor."The husband mouth was still drop open, from the doctor remarks, when Queen Sheba recited, " You

better close your mouth before a fly enter it, you have all ready let another fly's out of it, talking to old Dr. that way." His mouth close shut, like a draw bridge on a castle, looked at Queen Sheba, roll his eyes at her. The bus pull back onto the road, after all the confusion and false alarm, ten minutes later, the mother to be, utter to her husband, " Dear, I have use the rest-room again," he looked at her, with a smile, knowing he will get another drink of that refresher back there, took her hand, helping her out of the seat, look down in it, seeing the deflated balloon in it and angrily shouted, ! Which one of you kids, put that water balloon in my wife seat?" Stare at Joe and Sam, who answer at the same time, " Not me Mr." Then he looked at Queen

(26)

Sheba, who answer the same way," Not me Mr." The mother eye Sam with suspicion, as he turn his head to avoid her glances, so she couldn't

see his guilt in them, the husband and his wife, started down the aisle toward the rest-

room, she went in as Tiny hand her husband another cup of Tequila in it, smile looking

like horns was coming out the side of his head and mutter, " I warm you about father-hood, before the baby arrive." His wife came from the rest-room and they waddle, back down the aisle to their seats, Tim woke up, said to Tony, what was happening up front and why did the bus pull over to the side, or was I dreaming? Tony turn around in his seat, smile, answering " No Tim, you was not dreaming, the young lady up front, thought her baby was coming, Queen Sheba, with her partner in crime, Sam has struck again on an innocent by-stander, Tim put his head back on Gail shoulder and went back to sleep. Queen Sheba, tap the young lady on her shoulder, replying, " Don't worry honey, your baby will be in this world, before you get home." An hour later, the young bride woke up her husband and declare, " Honey, I think the baby is on its way now, I am having sharp pains, every five to ten minutes." Her husband jump up out of his seat, shouting at the driver, ! Its for real this time! Pull over, and where are you at Dr. Wallace? The Doctor, rise up out of his seat, pick up his black bag, slowly taking his time, started down the

aisle to the young mother, her husband holler out, ! Come on Dr! why are you walking

so slow? " With a smile, he gaze at her husband, utter in an soft voice, "Roman was not

build in a day and slow up. My young man it has taking mine mouths, for the baby to arrive, so what is your hurry? I knew you will be calling me soon, when I first examine your wife." Now see if there is anyone that have some blankets, that we can use, to hang up around her for our privacy. Queen Sheba, Pat and Lyn, with the Golden Gris, said they had some, the Dr. and her husband started hanging them up around the young mother, with Dr. Wallace going in with her, the husband stood on the outside. About an half a hour later, he hear a smack and crying on the other side of the blankets, with Dr. walking out saying you are a father of a nice baby boy, walk toward the rest-room, with his black bag. Queen Sheba looked at the young mother, with a motherly smile saying, " Well, its a boy." didn't I tell you, the baby will be here, in this world, before you get home." Tim and Gail woke up, after the bus had pull back on to the road ask Tony, what were they doing up fount, he turn, looked at Gail, said with a smile, the young mother up fount just deliver her baby, Tim gaze at Gail, with bed-room eyes, muse, " You want a baby Gail? She roll her eyes at him and snarl, " The only thing, that will come out of you, is alcoholic beverages and maybe some water, which you don't know about." The bus pull into Ogallala terminal, came to a stop, with the over head-lights coming on, waking up Tony and the other passengers, as he rub is eyes from sleep, and seen the young couples, departing off the bus, with their new born baby and some other passengers behind them. The driver declare, " We will only be here an half a hour, to load and um-load, " Tony

look at his watch, on Sunday, 1:00 A.M,
looked around to see who else was awake,
and seen Queen Sheba rise up out of her seat,
coming his way toward the rest-room, he
thought, she would be the only one awake,
at this time of morning. She pass him, and
mutter, " This is a good time to cuddle up in
that nest, of yours, bird-nest, " and close the
rest-room door, before he could say
anything, with his mouth hung open,
shaking his head, hoping she will get flush
down the toilet, this time, when she use it.
Queen Sheba

(27)

inter back out of the rest-room, with that
same enticing smile, in the half lit, darkness
of the bus, with her eyes showing white and
wide, her teeth, the same color of her eyes,
an a
luminous came across her face, as she
swagger to her seat and sit down. The bus
was
 back on the road and hour later and swirl to
the side of the road after an inpact, with
a doe (Female deer) and ran into a jagged
mountain rock on the side, waking up the
passengers, the driver, went out side to
inspect the damage. He came back on the
bus, announcing in a calm voice, to the
passengers, "We had a flat tire, everything
will be alright, you can count on that, so you
can relax and go back to sleep, it is only a

flat tire on the right side, there is a ski resort an half a mile from here, I can slow drive it there and call Denver, for help." He went back outside, as Big Jack and Poncho looked out of the bus front window, seen the deer laying in the road, Big Jack said to Tiny, " Look like we are, going to have venison(Deer meat) tonight fellows, Tiny will get the deer from outside and bring it in, put it in Poncho seat, while I distract the driver." Big Jack, started down the aisle, to the front door of the bus, walking quiet, so he would not wake up any passengers, with Tiny behind him, Big Jack went off the bus first, started talking to the

driver, " I think you better check the other side of your tires, they felt like they were
going down, that why I came outside to tell you." The two started walking around to the
other side, that gave Tiny a chance to run off the bus and pick up the small deer, bring it back on the bus and put it in Poncho seat, while he went into the rest-room and hid. .Everyone was still a sleep, accept Tony, who was laughing in a quiet tone of voice at them, the driver came back in looking around at his passengers and in the rear, seeing everyone was in there seats, sleeping, seen a movement in Poncho seat, but disregard it because the deer had Poncho sombrero on, pull down over his eyes and nose he sit down in the driver seat and slowly drove back onto the road with an full

moon, shining on it, as he stop the bus again, putting on his bright bean head lights and didn't see the deer, he have hit, scratching his head, thinking, he knew there was a deer laying out there, slowly drove onto his destination. Poncho, was in the rest-room sitting on the toilet seat, with sweat coming off of his forehead, from a little claustrophobia, that he didn't know he have, eyes wide in the darkness of the rest-room, he started thinking, I will be glad when this bus get to where it is going, so that I can get out of this rest-room and breath again, in a half an hour he hear, the bus finally came to a stop, at the ski resort. The driver went inside, as Tiny knock on the rest-room door, telling Poncho, that all is clear for him to come out, Poncho came out of the rest-room, with sweat still coming off of his forehead and complaining about the hard toilet seat, he had to sit on and the close quarter he had to deal with for an half a hour. They spotted a picnic table over by the resort, Tiny remove the deer out of Poncho seat, putting it on his shoulder, as the three, waddle down the aisle, pass the sleeping passenger, Tony still laughing at them, in the rear of the bus. They put the deer on the table, Tiny rise his hunting knife, to skin it, the deer eyes pop open and jump off the table, and ran out of sight, with Tiny scratching his head shouting, !That dam deer, was only render unconscious! " Than he look up and seen the full moon over the mountains and the ski slope, with the ski jumps saying, maybe that is were it belong, back out in the wilderness were life is peace and tranquility, with know one to devour you, for there enjoyment, Poncho looked at Tiny, utter, " You are right, Tiny, I think everyone, should leave things along and let nature take its course." Big Jack,

(28)

had another thought on his mind, it would have been nice to had deer, for dinner tonight, , the three walked back on the bus, sit down in their seats, with their thoughts still on deer

meat, pulling their hats, down over their eyes for the night. Tony looked, across at them

smile, saying to himself, I guess they are worn-out, with all their active tonight, trying to

eat that poor little deer, now the only thing it have worry about, is the deer hunters out there; good luck my little friend. The full moon shine, into Tim eyes, as he shook Gail awake saying,, with bed-room eyes again, " Are you ready for your baby now? Everyone is a sleep and this is a good time before we reach L.A. " Gail, wide eyes half open answer," Don't you ever give up," close her eyes back up and went back to sleep, with Tim, thinking to himself, she don't know what she is missing, with an opportunity like this, when I am not drinking and all dry out. Tony was still awake in front of them, thinking they love each other, they are like me and my wife, when we were young, I hope there love will still flourish, when they get to the age of maturity and know one or themselves, can brake the bond of love between them. He looked on the opposite side of the bus window, by the cowboys, seen a big tow truck, pull up along side the bus and the

driver got out, Tony felt the bus rise up on that side, with the cowboys still sleeping and the rest of the passengers he thought, they must of had there Tequila before going to sleep and gave the other passengers some, because know one felt the bus being lift up on that side. After the bus was back down, the tow truck had left, the driver came in and looked around at the passengers, sit down in the driver seat, pulling his cap off, rubbing his head, like he had just did a eight hour work shift. Two hours later, the bus pull into Denver terminal and came to an stop, to let off the passengers for Denver, and a change of driver, we only have another time to check the tires and load up other passengers, because of that deer accident, he said to the new driver. The new driver was back on the route, as he left out of the terminal, after checking his list of passengers and loading and unloading, he was headed back up into the mountains, after an hour leaving the lights of Denver, behind him, the passengers still sleep, accept Tony who was looking out the window and seen the full moon, shining above the mountains on the snow and stars dancing in the heaven, he thought it is peace-full and beauiful out here, this time of morning, looking at God creation, there is know artist like our maker who, design this, then close his eyes to go to sleep, a.dream, that keep intermittent in his mind about his wife in the hospital, with Intravenous needles in her arm and him holding her hand, saying we will fight this cancer together, he open his eyes wide when the moring sun hit them, rub them, look around, to see who else was awake and went into the rest-room, to use it, and went back to sleep. Queen Sheba, woke up with the high morning sun, glowing in her eyes and started toward the rest-room, passing other passengers still sleep, looked down on Tony, who was still a sleep, before she went into the rest-room, patted him in the middle of his head again, waking him up saying Good morning Bird-nest, you have a nice rest, " and close the rest-room door, Tony snarl though the door, !I thought they left you at the ski resort last night! Tim woke up, with his hollering and said, " She is working over time on you Pops, maybe you should give in a little," and laugh, Tony turn around in his seat, gaze at him, with an obnoxious expression on his face utter, " Maybe the next stop, is her last one," turn back around, with Tim going back to sleep, with a smile on his face. Queen Sheba, return back out of the rest-room and started back to her seat, turning around muttering to Tony, " Don't you just love me, Bird-nest," and sit down in her seat. Tony

(29)

thought, she is building her hopes up to high, or she is going though a middle age crisis and don't know how to handle it, he went back into the rest-room, to freshen up after the

half sleep and lax of rest, from the bus incident, with the cowboys, keeping him awake,

 and Queen Sheba torment him, his eyes was still half close from sleep, he pass Tim and

Gail, with their head together and the cowboys, still sleeping with there big hats, over there eyes, sit down in his seat and went back to sleep. Waking up an hour later, he notice a new passenger, in the aisle seat, by Poncho, who look like some kind of sale-man and look around to see who else was new, on the bus, seen Joe, with his brother and mother with baby sister, had left, he knew Queen Sheba was still on the bus, when she went to the rest-room this morning, intruding in his rest and started to dose, as he thought it look like she is going to have to find her another partner in crime, and drop off, back to sleep again. Pat eyes brink open, with morning sun and looked up fount and seen Joe and his mother had left the bus, and shook Lyn awake saying, " Lyn, My little friend Joe is gone, him and his mother must of have departed off the bus in Denver, I am going to miss that

Chapter 7

little fellow," Lyn, wiping her eyes from sleep and a irk expression on her face, was woke
up out of peace-full dream, for once since she had been riding on the bus gaze at Pat answer, " Is that, what you woke me up for, because Joe is no longer with us," and lay her head back up against the bus window going back to sleep, excuse me miss Queen Lyn and close her eyes also, going back to sleep herself. The driver announce, " We will be in Cheyenne Wyoming, in an hour, you have a hour to eat breakfast and freshen up, before your next call, while the bus is being service, leave your luggage on your seats, because other passengers will be boarding." Tim, woke up with the driver announcement, said to Gail, " We have an hour, to find a store open. "Gail looked at him as to say, he need a doctor, I wonder is that Dr. still on the bus and utter " Fool, go back to sleep, don't you know it is Sunday,

everyone, take a rest and that mean you to.".
The bus pull into Cheyenne terminal, came
to a stop, as the passengers for Cheyenne,
departed off the bus first, the other
passengers went in for their breakfast, Tim
pull up another energy, to get up out of his
seat, started walking to the fount of the bus,
with Gail behind him and Tony behind
them, they enter the station and seen the
restaurant, Gail pointed to an empty table
over by some pictures of cowboys in a rodeo
and a mechanical horse, about ten feet away
from it. She thought, as they were sitting
down, I hope no cowboy, want to ride that
thing, while we are eating, the three look at
the breakfast menu, when the waitress came
over to their table, " Are you ready to order?
" Tim, was the first to order, utter, " You
can give me the number three, eggs, bacon,
with the sausage and grits, with hash
browns, can you tell the cook, to put extra of
everything on my order and don't forget the
biscuits." Gail eyes, buck went around in
there sockets, with her face lighting up, like
a candle and a smile came on it, she thought,
he have started back eating again, maybe we
can have that baby, he want so bad. Tony
order, just a coffee and some eggs said, to
Gail, " It is to early in the morning to eat a
lot," she looked at him and said, Tim must
of not heard you" with a laugh, Tim looked
at her uttering " What so funny Gail?" Me
and Pops, was just talking about something,

looked up at the waitress saying, " I will take the number three to, without the extra, " seen the little cowboy, big Jack gazing at the
(30)
mechanical horse, thought, don't neither one of you even think about riding that thing. The waitress, came back with their orders, siting two plates in fount of Tim, gave Gail hers, with Tony, the two of them look at Tim plates, wondering if he will fnish all thatfood, in an hour. Tim, started with his breakfast, looking like a bull-dosser moving dirt, from one location to another, he was crewing so fast, that Tony thought, could his esophagus take the fast intake to his stomach, Gail gaze at him saying,"Slow down, Tim or you might swallow the fork, " and laugh. Tony, started back eating, look over at the wrong table, were Queen Sheba was sitting, they eyes, met again, she wink, while she was eating, he thought, that women must have eyes, all around her head, another enticing thought came into his mind, maybe she should try to straddle, that mechanical horse and get throw to were, she is going .and don,t come back on the bus, with them winking eyes of hers and smling face. After breakfast, everyone came out of the restaurant and heard,
the station intercom, "The bus 1270, is now loading at gate 11, have a nice trip and thank you for riding Grayhound." Tony was in back of Tim and Gail, with Queen Sheba in

back of him, so close that he could feel her breath, hot on his neck in the dead of winter, when they left out the gate, heading toward the bus, the wind pushing them up into the bus, with every step. Everyone went back to thier designated seats, suddenly Tim jump up and run into the rest-room and Tiny on the other side of the wall, heard a loud noise, with the bus thin wall vibrating, he call on the other side of it and asserted," Young cowboy, you could use a Rotor Rooter, you know that plumbing company, that make sure your pipes are clean of debris, don't flush that toilet, until the bus leave the station, or they will have to evacuate the inside and outside of the station."Everyone started laughing, including Gail and Tony, on the opposite side of the aisle, with tears coming out of their eyes, from laughing so hard. Tim re-enter back out of the rest-room, when the bus pull off, rubbing his behind and ease down in his seat next to Gail, saying to her, " I feel like a new born baby," she looked at him and smile uttering, "You should, with all of that alcohol coming out of your body and the food, talking its place, "Tim smile at her , laying his head on her shoulder, went back to sleep. Tiny, was listening at Gail thinking, maybe he should take the same advice about drinking what you don't suppose to drink, but in moderation and that include my partners, Tony, notice a new passenger about the same side of Big Jack the two could have been brothers by there pant length, in the seat by Poncho , on the aisle seat, who look like a salesman. The bus was back on the road, to its designated city's, everyone was awake now, the man who looked like a sale-man, turn and look at Poncho by him and Big Jack, with Tiny in back of him, thinking to himself, here is some sucker's, with a smile on his face muse, " My name is honest Lace Mc' King, what are you, three cow-poke's are call by? "I have just, what the doctor order for you and your partners in back of you, this product will erode all old age winkle, from your face and being back the youth back to it, so you can still catch them young cow-girl,s and ride them bucking house,s, and put strength back into your body parts were it suppose be, you fellows know what I am talking about, don't you? Tiny gaze at the sale-man, with an, inconceivable smile, utter," Is that medicine any good? Or how come you, have not taking your own remedy? Look like I see a few winkles around your eyes." He stop in the middle of his sale motivation talk, with a smile reply back to Tiny, " My good tall friend, it doesn't work in a day or two, you have to keep taking it, until the results are

(31)
visual," reach in his black business case, pull out a bottle, with the label saying Early-

Sun Remedy, for all illness and being back your youth. Tim gaze over at the sale-man, ask him, "Do it have any alcohol content in it? The salesman reply," No young man, liquid food for the body, to help you keep that youth, it is all nature ingredient., when he
hear that, Tim look at him like he was about to cry, burst out, !Then why are you on the bus trying to sell something, that don,t have the right ingredient in it, driver let him off at the next station. and see can he can find a few sucker there to sell that non- alcohol medicine, to, you drink it." The saleman looked at Phocho by him reply, I will not be offended by the little young man, he is just thrist from the long ride on the bus. Tony and Gail was laughing at Tim, when the salesman continue his salesmanship, saying, " Fellows I also have another wonder pill here that will take away that middle access from around you, pull out a bottle of pills, Tim burst out again, " Maybe you should take the
whole bottle, so you can loosing up that girder you have on, with Gail and Tony still laughing at him. The salesman just look at him, rolling his eyes, thinking he wish he would go to sleep, so I can finish those sucker off, Tim in a sincere voice said "" Cheer up little fellow, I was just joking with you, I didn,t mean to hurt your feeling," pull his cap over his eyes, with Gail saying, "

You do have some feeling for other people."
Phocho smile at him, ask " Are you marry,"
lace answer, with sad eyes, " Yes I am and
with eight children, "he pull out his bill fold
and picture start falling out of it like coins
coming out a casno slod machine, Tiny in
back of him eyes went around in its socket,
when he seen all of them pictures, falling
out, saying, How did a little fellow like you,
get all of them kids, can I see your pictures,
they are hard to see from here, the saleman
handed Tiny his bill-fold, Tiny started
looking at it, seen one woman with four kids
on one side and turn it over, seeing another
woman on the other side, with four kids, but
the other woman on the other side, didn,t
resemble the one on the opposite side, he
thought,, I wonder do they cook the same, to
hold on to that little pot belly saleman, or
that little fellow must be pretty good in bed,
shakeing his head, giving the bill-flod back
to lace, saying, how come the ladie on each
side don,t look the same. Lace the saleman
eyes lit up ,saying," Well a man have to lay
his head some where after work, I travel
from coast to coast and I have a wife on the
East coast, another one on the West coast,
each one has four kids, four and four make
eight, the picktures you seen with the nunber
on it is the youngest to the oldest, so I will
not get mix up." Tiny, thought, while he was
scratching his head about the two womens
and thinkinig of a word that match the

saleman, said to Big Jack, I am trying to find a word for the salemen.he asnwer," Tiny, he is a polyganous, that the word, and I will say it again, in capital letter,! POLYGAMOU, and all them kids don,t have to be his kids, pops maybe and mom baby." he was talking lound another for everyone on the bus to hear and all turn looked at the salesman., he stuck his tongue out at them and went back to talking to the cow-boys, with an artificial smile on his face, saying," I wouldn,t say that, like I said a man have to rest his head some were from traveling from coast to coast, so don,t jugde me." Tiny tap him on the back, utter " Your head do lot of resting, but your other parts are over work." Everyone in back, by the rest-room was laughing. Lace close his sale bag, pull his hat over his eyes to go to sleep, a dream came into his mind, about his wife,s and children, they had his legs tie up and a rope around him under a tree, one of wife was sitting on him, while the other one, was pulling his teeth out, the kids was pulling his hair out, laughing at him with each strange
(32)
of hair, as he was hollering, ! I love all of you, I just wanted a family, as the kids started throwing rocks at him, he was still hollering, !I just wanted a family and be love, he jump

up bushing his clothes off, like something was on them. Tiny .gaze at him saying, "What
the matter Lace, some of your un-satisfified customer, was throwing something at you in your sleep.? Tim looked at him, muse " What did you do dunk some of your medicine, you are selling? Then Tony ask him was he alright, Lace looked at Tim first, rolling his eyes and then answer, "Yes Mr, I just had a bad dream about my wifes and kids.," got up out of his seat, going into the rest-room.. Tony thought, with that clan, I don,t see how he rest any way,. Lace came back out of the rest-room and got conformable in his seat, taking his hat off, putting it in his lap, close his eye, to go to sleep. Tony thought, I gress his conscious is whiping him, with having them two wifes, Queen Sheba rise up out of
her seat and started toward Tony, on her way to the rest-room, he thought, here come trouble, but she stop at Lace seat, looking at Tony while waking him up, rubbing his hair and twisting her finger around it, whlie Lace was smiling like a puppy dog, being scratch by his master, Queen Sheba smile at him, then at Tony saying " Are you marry, with that cule smile?Lace put on more of a smile looking like the character, that play the role of the joker in the movie the Batman, he smile utter," You look like a lady I seen in a movie, "with more of a smile from ear to ear,

eyes shining like the north star, "Yes Mam,,
I am," and griming all the time, while she
was playing with his hair and   ,
looking at her pretty soothe black skin and
smiling at her, but before he could get
another word out, Phocho busted out, "Yes
Mam and with two wifes and eight kids",
Queen Sheba hurry up and took her hand off
his head, like she was burn by a hot iron,
said what do you have in them little short
pants of yours and walk into the rest-room,
still looking at Tony, who was thinking, she
is just trying to make me jealous, to see if I
will give her a play.. Queen Sheba came out
of the rest-room, troller back to her seat, turn
back around looking at Tony, wink her eye
again at him,, he turn his head and look back
out the window at the montain, terrain,
wishing the driver would put her off at the
bottem of them, and tell her she have to
walk the rest of the way to L.A, He look
back up front afther she had went to sleep,
then he look at the mother, and two kids,
one resting on her shoulder and the other
one, who resemble Sam, who have got off
the bus, at the last stop, he look about the
same age, with that same devilist smile on
his face, thought, look like Queen Sheba has
another parther in crime. Tony eyes were
getting heavy, he drop off to sleep and did
not see the kid getting up coming his way to
the rest-room, the cow-boys sleep to, the
kid look down an seen Tiny lasso hanging

half out of his bag on the floor, thought, he will have a good time, when he use the rest-room, after using it and came out, he Ben down and took the lasso out of Tiny bag, tie it to his seat and across the aisle to Tim seat, walk back to his seat. Phocho craw over Lace, to use the rest-room , rubing his eyes from sleep and this not see the lasso across the aisle, he trip over it hitting the back of the bus, smashing his sombrero, down on his head and eyes, to a cap side, as he took both hands try to pull it up off of his head, it finaily came loose and he walk in the rest-room cusring in his Mexican assent. Tony thought the devil has stuck again, Phocho came out of the rest-room, un-tie the rope looking at Tiny, saying, " Why don,t you close your bag, so no one can see, what you have in it", Tiny smile at him saying I throught you was in a rodio, the way you hit the back of the bus, was that a good horse that trew you? and laugh, with everyone else laughing. The driver, was keeping his eyes on the

(33)

road, thinking he will be glad when this trip is over, with all of those nuts on broad.. Big Jack tap Phocho, on the back, ask him, " Did he enjoy his ride " and laugh, he pull his sombrero down over his eyes and close them. Pat look at Lyn musing, "Darling I have to

use the rest-room," Lyn gave her one of them looks saying, "What you want me to do,
hold your hand? And whisper, make show you check your bag again for bugs and laugh, Pat just put her hat up in the rack walked off, not paying any attenion to Lyn remarks, when she got to Tiny seat by the rest-room, he blasted out !Wow hi there pretty mature Mom, were did you come from? You show look good to the eyes." Pat roll her eyes at him and reply my big gentle-man, " I am not your Mom and for two I would not be your Mom, at the size of you I hope she is still walking after having you and for three, that is
my business were I came trom, "Tim holler out ! That telling him lady" Tiny look at him him, with eyes saying close your mouth or I will close it and through his hand up at her
in a gesture of I did not mean any harm and repeat his words " You are stiill a pretty lady, Pat smile and stared pattering on her wig like it was real hair smilng, walk into the rest-room, Tony thought, Tiny buest her bubble he must not of been on the bus, when Sam shot that wig off of her head, I hope that wig is glue on good if thay get together or he will be looking at the full moon 'Pat came out of the rest-room, still smiling at Tiny as she try to wiggle what little she had, Tiny kept his eyes on her all the way to her seat, with the wrong kind of thoughts in his

head, she sit down by Lyn still rubbing her wig like it was real and said to Lyn, " Did,t I tell you I was a star, that big fellow in back can,t keep his eyes off of me," Lyn kept looking out the window saying in a smart way, "" Did he have a white cane or was he drunk," and laugh, Pat just look out the window with her at the scenery, thinking I will fool that old witch, when I get to Hollywood. The driver announce , We will be stoping at a rest-stop in about twenty minute, you have fifteen minutes to use the rest-room or search your legs, the mother look at her son , who was turning back and forward in his seat looking at people ask him, ""Why are you wiggering so much in your seat Frank? He answer, "Noning mom, just looking at the people on the bus,"Tony heard his name, and throught, it should have been Sam two, they have the same spril in them, with the same devilish smile on his face, the bus came to a stop at the rest-stop, everyone started un-loading, all of them was off the bus, when Frank said to his mother, "" I have to go get my cap mom, it is hot out here." his mother ansswer,"Go a head and get it and come right back here," Frank went back on the bus looking on the seat and up under it, spoted it, with a tump tack laying by it that the bus maintance chew miss when they last clean the bus, he pick up his cap and the tack, wondering what to do with it, look over where the young men was sitting

there and put it in the scat by the window,
walk off the bus.The driver said it was time
to load back up and everyone   started back
on the bus, with the two young fellows, in
there loud color shirts on, still talking, as
the driver call them, they started in,
everyone else was sitting down, as one stay
in the aisle, to let his pardner in, by the
window, as he sit down and jump up with a
holler,! I sit on something sharp in my seat,
hollering at his pardner,   ! hurry up and
.pull it out!, his pardner had his hand over
his mouth, to keep from laughing while
everyone on the bus was laughing, he pull
the tack out of his rum and blood shot out
like someone opening a champagne bottle
cork, hitting him in his eye his pardner, half
ran and wiggler in them skin tight blue jean
he had on to the rest-room, when he got to
Tiny seat with him saying" What do we
have here?, he just looked at him rolling his
(34)
eyes and went in the rest-room, Tim said to
Tiny, "It dosen make you any diffence who
you flirt at ,do it." Tiny gase at him with
another look of keep on being smart, said
"My little cow-boy, your drinks are cut off
for real this time ", Tim looked at Tiny,
uttering, "
 Now, you know I was just playing with you
buddy," Gail was sleep and did not hear Tim
pleasing for a change of mind on Tiny. Tony,
thought, Tim got out of that problem with

Tiny in a hurry and laugh to himself. While the young man was in the rest-room, that had a small winodow in it, that no one could see out of or in, a bright light shine across his face and he hear a voice saying What God created you to be, is what you must be, not what you want to be, but what God want you to be, at the same time his body was feeling
 the muscular strengh coming in it and all other feeling and disire of the body, was
 dispearing. He walk out of the rest-room and stop at Tiny seat, ask him in a huskey voice
"What did you say, when I was going into the rest-room".Tiny thur his hands up again with that juster of I did not say a word, as the young fellow walk off, without the wigger,Tony thought the Lord work in mystery ways as his pardner rise up out of his seat to let him in to the window seat and set down as his pardner ask him "Are you alright dear", he reply back rolling his eyes, said," Do I look like, I have anthem coning out of my head," and look out the window, his pardner thought, look like I have got to find me another freind when I get to L:A, he has became a man again.The driver annouce, "We will be in Albuquerque New Mexico in a hour, the ones who are not getting off, put your bags in your seat, because other passengers will be broading, you have a hour there to get you, a little something to

eat.Tiny look at Tim, who who was shaking all over his body, said, "I will take care of you little cow-boy, when we get back to the bus, if we have another time, to get the shakes off of us all," Lace was listering and thought,all of you need to drink my medicine, utter " 'You fellows need to take my remedy." Tim holler out, !We have toke you, to drink it yourself."Lace, just laugh and gaze at Phonco, who had blood shot eyes, with a smile saying,"You look like a fellow who know what good for him, try it and you will feel better." Phonco, had enother enery to tell lace, my horse woild not drink that stuff. Lace turn around in back of him saying to Big Jack, "You look like you are in the same boat, they are, maybe you should try some," .Big Jack kelp looking out the winodw and thinking he must be insane if he think I am going to drink that so call medcine. Lace turn back around thinking, all of them will learn what they are doing to there mind and there bodys The bus came to a stop in Albuquerque station, the passengers in front, started unloading first and the back came up behind them, with Lace, Phonco and Tiny,carrying his over-night bag, then Tim and Gail, with Tony, thinking about Tiny and his bag, he is going to load up, for the rest of the trip, all of them look like they been at an over night party and just got off their horses from a long ride, Lace was carrying his sale bag

also, Tony thought, I gust he think that he
will find some sucker in the station. They
seen the restaurant and walked in, and seen
the cow-boys headed to the front doors Tiny
look across the street and seen a liquor store
said, we are in luck fellows, there is a store,
right across the street. Tim, Gail and Tony
was sitting togerther at one table, Tony look
over and seen Lace sitting across to the right
at another talble, with his products on top of
it, Tony thought, he have to hurry up and
sale that product, to feed them two faimlys
and laugh to himself, with Gail asking him,
what he was smiling about, noning Gail, just
thinking about something, look at the other
side of the room,

(35)
seen Queen Sheba sitting at a table by a
mechancal bucking horse, , winking again,
he, thought, she is not going to be able to
open them eyes one day if she keep on
winking, I
hope she get on that horse, so it can throw
her to L.A. The Golden Grils, with Pat and
 Lyn, was stitting together talking, Tony
thought, now that cule all the mature ladies
together. Big Jack, Tiny and Phonco came in,
sit down at another table by the mechancal
horse, Big Jack look at Tiny " Saying I bet
you ten dollars, I can ride that horse until the
battery run out " , Tiny said, " You on and
pay up, if you get throw off". Big Jack went,

got up on the horse, with his little short legs
hanging down, because they could not reach
the saddle steep, he put his change in the
slop, the horse started bucking with him
holding on to the head shape and waveing
his ten gallon hat with one hand hollering,
he was on it about ten minute with eveyone
one watching with their hands over their
mouths hoping he hurry up and get off that
horse, while he was holding the other shape
with one
hand, broke, throwing him on the floor, that
had been just wax and he slide up under the
soloom doors of the kitchen, you could hear
pots and pans falling, as he walk out the
kitchen, bushing his clothes off, with food
all over him, and everyone laughing, he
went in his pocket and pull out a ten dollar
bill, thru it in front of Tiny, who was just
smiling, saying, " Don,t say a word".
Phocho, just put his hand over his mouth,
to keep from laughing, turn his head to
another view. Tim holler over to the table, !
I Thought you were a cow-boy, or are you
one of them Hollywood cow-boys?, Big
Jack answer back, " Can,t win them all.".
The in-com came on, " The bus for El Paso
Texas is boarding at gate 9, have a nice trip
and thank you for riding Grayhound,
everyone headed to gate 9, with Big Jack
leading, rubing the not up under his ten
gallon, from his ride, Tiny look at him utter
" Let me see your head," Big Jack bent his

head over and Tiny said, ! wow, you have a good one there, but you will live, just don,t ride your horse like that, when we get home" and smile, with Big Jack smiling to. All the passgener that was on the bus, set down in there seats, with other passengers broading and a new driver came in annoucing the rules of Grayhound and his name, Tony seen that the mother and her two boys did not come back on, thought this must have been there stop, I hope she find a priest, to gvie Frank a exorcist and Sam mother, did the same thing, they, need one bad, before they grow up, why each driver come on, annouce the rules of the bus, they must be talking about the front and not the back, if they only knew what go on back here, every body will be walking and smile. The bus went back on the road and Tony hear bottle caps coming off Tiny said to Big Jack, " We are all most home fellows to the open range, away from these city folks, so let us have our last party," started passing out cups of Tequila to everyone, but Lace and Tim, who said, " Were is minds," with his eyes on Tiny cup and body shaking,, with Gail looking at him, rollering her eyes, Tiny gaze at him with a smile saying " Did,nt I tell you, your drinks was cut off," Gail thought good, I hope the bottle will brake on all of them, Tiny then pour Tim a cup, saying, " You know I was just playing with you, little cow-boy and you know you still my buddie ,make sure there is not a worm in it this time", and laugh, a grin came on Tim face, while he reach for the cup, Gail, still rollering her eyes at him. . Tim look down in the cup, to make sure a worm was not in it and smile turning it up to his mouth, Tony thought, here we go again, until the bottles are empty, Tiny patted Lace, on the back saying, " You want a cup, fellow, you look as doe it will eliminate, your thinking about selling them products and get on with your life," Lace said, " Never mind, I will drink my own remedy", Tiny utter,"

(36)

That is a good idlea, since konw one else will drink it," and laugh, Phonco mutter out "Maybe you should drank that stuff, so it will cut down on your fertilization, because you been to actist, you can,t help get all the babys in this world," and laugh,. Lace gaze at

Phonco, with little tear at the corner of his eye saying " You fellows talk about my life syle, I am like everyone else in this world, loving and caring for the ones who love me and I love them, I never had to many friends, when I was growing up and still don,t, staying mostely to myself, is a longely job, but I survival it, all of you I, thought this was

at begaining of friendship, but I gress I was wrong, look up front with sad eyes. Phonco

looked at him with series eyes saying,"We was just treasing you, we do everyone like that, that is our bubby, don,t feel bad, it is just our way of showing frindship, we like you
 for our pardner," then Big Jack but in , Phonco right, cheer up, we will be off at the next stop and we will miss you, trying to sale us your home make remedy and laugh. Tiny follow in saying, " They are right little fellow," Tim but in saying," That right Lace, you are our buddy", Lace put a smile on his face, that said thank you fellows. Tony was listering to them, started thinking about the world of people, saying to himself, they are right in a way,we live in a world, were you have to hold on tight to what or who you have and what belong to you, it is to bad that man or woman, have to share themself, but that is their choice of living, not God doing, but their, while they are in the wallls of their body, that inplane things in your mind, that is not suppose to be there, like when to say things at the right time and not to say things at the wrong time,or keep it close, for words are happyness and a weapons, he look back up front, seeing Pat, Lyn and the Golden Girls, still talking, then, the wrong way across the aisle and met Queen sheba eyes again, with her smiling, winking and, blowing a kiss at him, with her hand, he throught, is she ever going to give up, I hope someone will come on this bus, who will

satisfy her need, and look   were the two young mens was setting togather, the one by the window, had move to another seat across the aisle by the Golden Girls, Tony thought again, I gress their relationship is broke up, he must have got a good dose of something when he last went to the rest-room. A lady was setting by the one on the aisle now and him by the window, Tony said to himself, she don,t have to worry, about   him and smile , turning looking out the window. Big Jack was listering at Phonco and trying to laugh, but his head was hurting, with him rubbing the not on his head, ask Tiny pour him some more Teqiula in his cup, maybe my head will stop hurting Tiny said," let me see your head, it is going to be alright" I hope you don,t ride your own horse that way, when we get home." The driver annouce, " We will be in El Passo in a half an hour, the ones who are going on to Phoenix Arizona, put your bags in the seat, because other passgners will be broading, you have an hour lay over and thank you for riding Grayhound." all of the back was looking at each other like they were about to cry, Tony thought, it just like being in the service, were everyone part from their buddies and go a diffence way, maybe it is best for some people to go another place and you some were else. The bus pull in to El Passo station and stop,and the driver went out side by the door, the front started unloading first with

the passengers leaving, Tiny, Phonco and
Big Jack, went in their bags pull out gun
hoster, with 45 pistol in them and scalp them
on , Tim eyes roll around in his head, saying
!Wow, they sure are pretty,"Tiny look at
him saying it is legal to carry them out west
as long as they can be seen, Tony thought,
he had another of weapons in the service and
there is another of them out here in these
city's, that are killing up each other and the
kids,

(37)

who don,t have time to grow up to enjoy life.
Gail looked at Big Jack, laugh, when she
seen the way his holster was on him, up high
on his waist and hanging low on the other
side down by his thigh, with the 45 pistol in
it. They look at Tim, Gail and Lace saying
good by, city folks, we are on our way to
the open country, were life is peacefull and
 you take care of that gal Tim, because she
love you, Gail put a skile on her face, with a
 tear starting in her eyes, you to Pop,s, as the
kids call you, Tony just smile, wave to

                              Chapter 8
them, they started down the aisle to the door,
^Tim, put is fingers up like he had pistols
and holler at Tiny, !Draw,' Tiny,spin around,
like he only weight a hundred ponds and
drew his pistol out of his hosters, like a flash
of lighting and wiggle them around on his

finger and rehoster them, Lace had junp up
in his seat, Tim said !Wow, you are fast,"
Tiny reply back,, "That the way it was in the
old west, these day, they are only for show".
Big Jack, try to indated Tiny with his pistol,
swirh it around on his finger, but it got in the
tirigger, shoting himself in the foot, he
holler !My foot, my foot," The driver out
front holler in the bus !Who is shooting fire
chacker on the bus". Tiny look at Big Jack
foot and said " Didnt I tell you about trying
to imitate me, now look what you have did,
Tiny said to him " Sit on the seat arm rest,"
he took off his boot and warp his bankdana
around his foot, picking him up like a baby,
stated carrying him to the bus front door,
The driver gaze at him saying what wrong
with him, Tiny reply , he just shoot himself
in the foot, I am taking him to the doctor
now, we will come back and get our other
bags. Phonco had all the over-night bags,
draging them behind him, The driver looked
at them and pull off his cap , started
scratehing his head, they went toward a city
cab out front The driver thought, I hope they
didn,t put a big hole in the bus floor. Gail,
Tim and Tony was the last ones off the bus,
passing the driver, still laughing, at Big Jack,
as they walked into the station, the driver
went back on the bus, drove off to the
station garage, thinking, he will be glad
when he get to Phoenix, were the other
driver will relief him, so he can get away

from these nuts. Tim spotted a restaurant over to his left, said to Gail and Tony, let eat, I am hungry, Gail look at him saying you are ready to eat now, sent your buddies are gone and smile. They frond a table and sit down, Tony sarted looking around to see who was in there, seen Pat, Lyn and the Golden Girls still talking, he wonder, how can they find so much to talk about from one city to the next, then at Queen Sheba, who was still winking, he thorught, that he wish there was a clothe pin around so that\ he could put on her eye lids and pin them down, he seen the two young men sitting at opposite tables, said to himself, they have not may up yet, there is still a long way to go, maybe they will be back buddies again, what ever their difference call for..Tim order from the waitress, two sandwish and france frys and a salad, as Gail said to him, you are hungrey and laugh, the waitress cane back with Tim order and he started eating like he had not eaten in a mouth, as Gail kelp looking at him eating, with a smlie on her face , looking up, Tony gaze at her , knowing what she was during, praying and thinking the Lord, he wa eating again..After Tim taking his last bite, he jump up runing to the rest-room, Gail said," Food run through him, like water", Tony laugh.. When Tim went in the rest-room all the toilet stales had out of order signs on them , he look around to see were he could go, than peep out the door, to see if anyone was looking and a may a quick dash to the woman rest-room, hopeing there was know lady in there and went to a toilet stale,

locking   it , sitting down on the toilet getting a relief, two ladies came into the rest-room talking, Tim put his feet up on the toilet, were they could not see them in the stale, they stay about twenty minutes talking, Tim was sitting in a awkward position on the toilet,

sweating at the same time, because the air condition, was not working to good, they

finality left and he came out of the stale, look around and peep out the door to see if

anyone was looking, may a quick dash out the woman rest-room. He went back to his table and sit down, Gail ask him what taking him so long, it is almost time to load back on the bus, he look at Gail with a silly look on his face. The in-com came on for the bus to Phoenix, AZ is boarding at gate 8, Tim just kelp that silly smile on his face, they started walking to gate 8. They all boarded back on the bus, taking their bags back up out of the seat, sit down, with Tony looking back up front, seeing a elderly man with a black clergy suit on and a white collar around his neck, when he reach the young man with the long pony tail and loud color shirt on, he just threw his hand up in the air, sit down in back of him and started reading his bible, sill shaking his hand in the air. Tony smile, thought he should of been back here when the cow-boys was here, he reality would, of had a hold lot of souls to save, with them, lace and Tim, included, he look back up front again, seening Queen sheba eyes, getting ready to wink again, he put up his finger , waving it from side to side saying don,t wink them eyes, she smile, turn around in her seat.. The driver came in dictating the rules of the bus as always and his name. The bus pull off on the road to Phoenix.. Pat utter to " Lyn I have to use the rest-room darling, Lyn look at her and said, " Why are you telling me all the time when you have to use the rest- room,? do I look like your husband," Pat just thru her hands up in the air and thought, she a hope-less case and wiggle off to the rest-room, .with a smile on her face, that drop off thinking the big cow-boy was there, but he was gone, she throught, I didn,t get a real chance to meet him, The other man in the seat smile at her,, she said " Whit that smile off your face, you are not the one I wanted to see," and went into the rest-room. , Tony throught, well Miss lady, your bubble burusting days are over for right now, she came back out of the rest-room, ask Lace were was the big cow-boy, ,he look at her with sad eyes, because he miss them to, saying they got off in El Passo,. She just walk into the rest-room, Tony thought, there go her love afair and smlie. Pat came out of the rest-room, with the smlie still off of her face, watk down the aisle not wiggling, sit down, thinking she can,t have all the men, but he was cule ,and he did reorganize me as a star, Lyn intercede into her thought, saying, " Are you relife now, did you see your big cow-boy back there, who think you are a star?, Pat reply back, "Yes I am and their was no cow-boy back there, Miss smartly, " close her eyes, before Lyn could get another word out. They was on the open road now, as Tim eyes started to close, he went to sleep,. dream land enter his mind, becoming a night-mare, with him tie to a tree and all kind of liquor brand bottles with heads and little legs on them, they tape open his mouth, took their head off and started, pouring there content in his mouth, then the worm that he drink in the Tequila that Tiny gave him,was growing in his stomch and getting larger, and larger, like a pregnant woman, it burst open, with little baby liquor,bottles coming out of him, with heads and litte legs on them to, the little liquor bottles, untie him, started draping him to the grave yard, Saying you are coming with us to the grave, he was

(39)

hollering, ! Please, I don,t want to go, please, I have to stay with Gail,! they said, " You

must go, if you don,t quit miss using us, "
Tim started back hollering again,! I quit,, I
quit, please let me go back to Gail!. and
holler, !Gail help me,! help me Gail!. He
was shaking and thowning his head from
side to side, Gail woke him up, telling him,
he was having a night-mare, with eyes wide
open he look like he had just seen a spirit
with his eyes, sparkling like the mid-day sun ,
he said I have to use the rest-room, still in a
daze,
 got up and went into the rest-room, with
Gail still looking at him, wondering what
was
he dream about.Tony hear them, ask Gail,
what was wrong with Tim, Gail answer, " I
don,t know Pops, I been wondering,
because he stop drinking for a while, with
the cow-boys, maybe he is taking a new
lease on his life, Lord I hope so". Tony
utter," He will be alright, just take it slow
and don,t worry, he will make it," Gail with
a little tear coming out of her eyes, said, " I
hope you are right Pops." While Tim was
sitting on the toilet, a bright light shine on
his face, not from the rest-room, because the
window was the kind that you could not see
in or out, at that time of day, it was still light
out side, Tim did not cut the lights on when
he went in, a voice came out of the light
saying , "You don,t defile my body, that I
created, it is not yours to use any man
substance, that I gave   some of my

knowledge to make for his surival, along time ago, not to use for bad, only good".Tim rise up off the toilet in a daze look around to see where he was at, his body, started to feel different inside and the shakes was gone out of it, he walk out the rest-room, sit down,,   Gail look at him staring out in shape and ask him " Are you alright," Tim answer "Yes Gail, I just know what I have to do from now on, go to sleep and rest yourself and stop worring about me, everything will be alright." She lay her head back on the head rest   thought what do he mean by them remark and close her eyes,Tony hear them, said to himself, she don,t know what he is going though, but I do, his body is going though a change and trying to rebuid it self back to normal, I konw, because, I been there and back, it will take him a lot of will power to brake the hibit and stay on the right track, I hope that everyone who have some kind of habit, will have the will power to brake it and live there life, the way that the Lord intent for them to live, he lay his head back on the head rest and went to sleep, like some of the people on the bus.The driver annonce "We will be at a rest-stop in about twenty minutes, before we go on to Phoenix, which is about another hundred mile from there, so you can have a brake in riding so long." Lyn look at Pat saying" Let me out, I have to use the rest-room, you have me going, much I see you

go" ,Pat rise up out the seat, to let her out
and repeated her words, what you want me
to do , hold your hand and laugh, Lyn, just
roll her eyes, walk to the rest-room, in about
ten munties she return out, walk back to her
seat, as she sit down Pat ask her, """ Did she
see any cow-boys back there," and laugh
again, Lyn, just ignor her and look back out
the window.The bus, pull into the rest stop,
Tony look out the window to see cactus, all
around the stop on the other side of the bus
they where arrang in circles, standing about
five or six feet in hight, him and Gail, with
Tim   and   Lace,   following   the   other
passingers off the bus. Most of them was on
the passengers side of the bus at pienick
tables Tony spoted some picnick tables on
the opposite side, Gail ask them do they
want something to drink, they mutter, yes, it
is still hot out here, and   the sun is almost
down, , all of them   sit down where, all the
catus was in a ciricles, Gail went to get
something to drink, they started talking and
seen Gail coming back with two bottles of
water in each hand and one bottle of water
each, up under her arm pit, Lace and Tim
seen

 (40)

her, ran to help her, when they got to her
she said, "What were the two of you runing
about, I have carry more then this at home,"
they all sit down, drinking there water, when
Tim jump up running toward the bus, Gail

said," There he go again " Tim could not make it to the bus, but ran in between the ciiricles of catus, that was wide another for him to get though them as he pull his pants down to do what had to do, a ratter shake junp out a hole on the other side of the catus and was getting ready to strike at him making him back into

a catus, its prickies penetrated his butt, he holler, pull up his pants, ran from between them toward the other side of the bus, waving at Gail, who jump up follw him to the bus, everyone look at him, wondering what was wrong with him, holding his pants up, Tim went to the back of the bus, were know one could see him from the outside, Gail came in, he holler,! !What took you so long", pulling his pants down, Gail look, started laughing saying," You look like a porcupine from the rear", Tim utter, "Will you please started pulling these thing out before someone come on the bus," Gail started pulling them out one at a time, singing a music time at the same time, a one and a two and a three, and a four, Tim jump with each pull, holler at the same time, like he was in tone with her timing, when she was though, he went in the rest-room to clean up, when he came back out, Gail ask him did he want to go back outside with Pops and Lace, still haghing, Tim said " No, it is almost time to come in any way", Gail just walk to the door, as Tim holler,! You better not tell anyone what happen"., Gail look at him, still laughing, than went out the bus door, back to Lace and Tony, but before she could say anything, as they were getting ready to ask her about Tim, the driver said " It was time to load up, everyone loaded back on the bus, sit down, Tim was still holding his finger up to Gail, to keep her mouth close, she smile. The driver pull back out on the road., as the young man with the loud color shirt on and pony tails, got up out of his seat, across from his use to be buddy, walking toward the rest-room in a mannerly matter, with his over-night bag in his hand, about twenty minutes he return out, with a solid color shirt on, his pony tails were gone, sit back down in his seat, his pardner look at him and smile, the two close their eyes and went to sleep. The bus pull into Phoenix station, stop, the bus driver said "We have an half a hour here to load up, you can stay on the bus or get out and loosing up your legs, from riding, while we are unloading and loading,"After an hafe a hour, the bus was back on the road again, a full moon was hoovering over the mountain tops, waking up Queen Sheba, by the bightness of it, also Tony, hitting his eye lids as he look up front, seening Queen Sheba, ponting at it, smiling, he thought, Miss lady, you are not going to put your pangs in me and draw my blood, close his eyes again, going back to sleep. The morning sun woke up Tony, with most of the passengers still a sleep in front and back, he rise up out of his seat, went into the rest-room, looking around, like he expect to see something, he must have been in good standard with what or who ever was in there, when the young men and Tim went in. He came out, Tim and Gail said," Good morning Pop,s," Tony greet them back with a good morning, look at Lace, who was still sleeping, like he had a hard days work, selling his products.. About two hour later, of riding, Tim got out of his seat, kneel down on the bus floor on his knees putting his arms on the arm rest of the seat, look at Gail, Pat so happen to turn around to look in the back, seeming Tim on his knees, saying " Lyn what is that young man doing on his knees? Is he , praying,?" Lyn gaze at her utter " No silly, he is getting ready to propose to his young lady, don;t you know when someone is praying or not? Pat look at her,said " Let see it you are right

(41)

"..Gail look back at Tim gazing at her, wondering what is on his mind, Tim said in a soft voice, " Gail, I know that I have put you though a lot of things, making you cry, and worry about me, I was only thinking about myself, with the problems that I have, but all of that will change, because my body is getting back to normal, you are the only one I want and need, to think about, you are my world, I could not of myself may it this

fare, I love you Gail, I been wanting to ask you this for a long time ". Gail said, with her eyes
sparkling, like sapphire," What is it Tim?. he muse, " Will you marry me Gail,"She jump
up out of her seat, grape him around his neck, while he was still kneeling, gave him a big kiss, uttering ," Yes, yes Tim, I been waiting for this along time" kiss him again, .Lace and Tony, with everyone on the bus chapping their hands, with little tears coming out of Pat eyes, Lyn said, ' You not getting marry, what you crying about? Tony reply, " I thought you two were all ready marry? Tim said " No Pops, we were just staying together ".Tony thought, it the same way him and his wife did for a while, before we did the real thing, maybe it is best for all couples to do it that ways, so they can find out about each other before making a mistake, and their love is out the window, marriages is not a game it is a two way street, that the two of you must go down, knowing each other emotions and moods, they will make it when they learn each other also respect the other ways..Tim holler, ! Is there a preacher on the bus," the little man that been reading his bible, send he been on the bus answer,"I am at your service, then started preathering to everyone on the bus, saying " My name is Preacher Tom, I am here to save your souls, all of you sinners from your evil deeds of living in this world,

that the father created for you, and to save all of you from the disaster that you are headed to, without God in your mind and heart, you sinners are in real trouble, when the Lord return for your sins and deeds of eivl in this life, if you don,t change your ways of living, pattering the young man, with the phony tail, on the shoulder and looked at him when he said that, started back preacthing, "You will regret, you were created in the image of God.". . Tony was thinking, Tim and Gail should of waited until thay got to L.A amd got marry, because when he get though preahering we will be there, he been at it for twenty minutes now, trying to covert peoples.The preacher turn, walk down the aisle toward Tim and Gail, ask them are you ready you two sinners, then ask Tim did he have a ring and license Tim mouth was hang open from his approach of words, started to say something, but change his mind, went up in the luggage rack, pulling his army jacket down, going in the inside pocket, getting a ring, with the llicense, Gail looked at him saying with amazement,, " How long had you have them?, Tim answer, "" They been in my pocket a long time, waiting for the right time to spring my love on you , when everything was right with me,"then ask Tony, will he best man, Tony said, " Anytime Tim" went an stood in back of him, Gail call out do anyone want to be my flower maid, Queen

Sheba jump up hollering, ! Here I come," as she look up, seen Pat hat, with the flowers around it, pull it down and started pucking the flonwers off of it, with Pat mouth gap open like it was lock in place, she walk down the aisle toward Gail and Tim, Lyn look at Pat, laughing, utter, " There go your star hat" and kept on laughing. Queen Sheba, went, stood in back of Gail, grab Tony hand, as he try to pull away, but she had a good grid on it , he was frowning at her, thinking, she do a have soft hand and shook his head of thought, that might come wrong in his mind, because, my wife is at home, waiting for me, she kept on smiling at him..The preacher look at Tim and Gail, ask, "Why do you two sinners want to get marry? Tim rolled his eyes at him, which

(42)

he did, not see and he continue, are you in love the right way with each other ? Or is it just your hunan body, with all of it desires that want you to get marry, are you ready and in love the right way, with each other or is a game to satisfy your desires, that make you think that you want to get marry ?. Tim started to say something again, but didn,t say it, Tony thought again, maybe they should of waited until, they got to L.A. The preacher started off with are there anyone, that have any deny about this marriage, speak now or

Chapter 9

for ever hold your peace. Lace holler out from his seat ! Will you hurry up and marry them kids, before they change their mind, then you will be the sinner, Tony said to Lace, " Thats my man, tell him again," The preacher put his glass on, look up under them at lace and Tony, turn back to Tim and Gail, started the marrage rite, at the end, I prounouce you sinner and sinner, oof, I mean huband and wife, with a little more to it, saying " Don,t let any man or wonam or your self or the world brake God bond bewteen the two of you, because God bond you together as one and that the way it should, be at the end of your days. Tim grap Gail and gave her a big long kiss, Queen Sheba said to Tony, "You want one to?, he reply back, " No thank you." Gail and Tim sit down in their seats, holding hands, still kissing each other, as Queen Sheba, thu the flowers in the air, it landed on Lace, Tony thought, he don,t need any more wifes, Queen Sheba, let his hand go, pinch him on the butt, as he jump, graping his rear end, she walk away saying, you have a soft behind for a man, laugh, sitting down in her seat. Tony sit down, wishing the driver would put her off at the next stop. The preacher walk back to his seat, with his bible open to read,. Tony thought, that preachter, do have the right points of life in his head, maybe that why God, appointed him to be one of his serant to the peoples. The bus went pass the California broader and now was in California, the other young man with the loud color shirt on with tight blue jeans on and a long phony tail, rise up out of his seat, grap his over-night bag, look at his use to be parther across the aisle, smile then walk toward the rest- room, with a little wiggle in his walk to clean up, while he was looking in the mirrow, a bright light came across his face, a voice saying " know who you are, you can not change what I created you to be, I am the maker of you, and all creation, so look at yourself good and know yourself, also me and understand, what I am saying ".The light disappear .and the voice, he stood there in a daze, looking at himself in the mirrow, thought, that is not me, then went in his bag and found a pair of scissors, started cutting off his phony tail, change his shirt, to a solid color one, pull off his thigt jeans off, with a little trouble and walk out the rest-room, back to his seat, without the wiggle, sit down, still in a daze, his parther look at him, thinking he must of hear something in that rest-room like I did and smile. The preather   look at him, in fount and thought, with his hand up in the air shaking it and looking up saying to himself, well lord we have another one coming back. Tony look at the preacher, said to himself, there go that preacher praying for someone, thought again look like the other young man, had an experence in that rest-room, I guess it

is your life stye that you are in, that being
out what ever is in that rest-room, I did not
see any thing when I went in there, maybe I
was clean.. Pat utter out to lyn, " You know
honey, I have came to the conclusion about
this profession, of lieing to peoples about
being hungry or I need to catch a bus, or I
have children at home who are hungry, just
to get there money that they work for, I been
thinking, it is not right, " with a serious look
on her face Lyn reply back " You know Pat,
(43)
I have been thinking the same thing, we are
getting to old for this, hustering off of
people, maybe we should retire from this
profession of begging peoples out of their
money and get something to do beside that."
Pat look at her with wide eyes saying " I
know you not talking about working, oh
know honey, I am to fare up in age for that ",
the two started laughing. The preacher hear
them talking while he was reading his bible,
put his hand up in the air, shaking it, look up
and said to himself ,Lord
my God, here come two more sinners back
to you, we will have them all soon, started
back reading his bible. Queen Sheba, pat the
preacher on the back saying "You profound
the kids, a nice wedding," he utter "Thank
you mam ",then she went on with her
conversation, " Are you marry preather
man," he said no, she continual "Well my
good man, all of us need to be love some

time, know matter what proffession you in, saving soul or not, as long as you are in that human body, you need love and smile," his eyes buck at her and ask her,"What is all those beans around your neck for, to reprsent your home land,? she said, "No preacher man they are voodoo beans, for your distiny in this life.", he hurry up and got out of his seat, pull his over-night bag out the rack, went to a seat on the other side of the bus that was vacant by the Golden Girls, open his bible up, thowing his hand back up in the air, shaking if, saying to the Lord within himself, Lord, we have a sinner here that we have a lot of work to do on, Queen Sheba kelp smiling at him..Tony was looking at her when she was talking to the preacher, wondering what she is saying to him, I hope he have lot of holly water to go on him while she was talking, and what did she say to him, that may him move so fast to the other side of the bus, we better hurry up and get to L.A, before she terrist someone else on this bus, she need a exorcist to, there is something in her, that is not right..The driver annouce" We will be in Santa Anna in about an hour,we will only be there, long another for to unload the bus and load, you can get off and rest your legs or stay on the bus.Tony look out the window, seen the sun going down and close his eyes,when he woke up the bus was pulling into the Santa Anna station and park, the passengers was getting their bags, leaving off the bus, as the last one left, others begin to load on, Tony notice a young man,with bluu jeans on and white shirt on, with white gym shoes, and no over- night -bag, coimg on stretching himself with each step he may,Tony look at him stretching, thought, I know what wrong with him, my son had the same symptom from lack of dope,. He walk up to the vancunt seat on the other side of Lace, , ask him to let him in to the seat, Lace move, let him in, still stretching as he sit down, Lace still trying to sell his product said," "Try my medicine young man, it is good for everything, that the body need, including a tonic" the young man gaze at him, with his eyes dilating, ask Lace, those it have any dope in it to make me high, lace utter back. "No young man, it is just naturally may, with no alcohal in it or narotic, it work on the body to get it back the way it was when you were born ". The young man just gaze at him with his eyes still dilating. The bus pull out of the station, back on the road, after about a half hour of riding, the young man ask Lace to let him out, so he could use the rest-room.. Lace move, look at him with his eye still dilating and looking wild, Tony look at him to, he went into the rest-room. He took his belt out of his pants, wrap it around his arm, ,pulling it tight, so his vains would be visual, reach in his other pocket pullimg out a hypodermic needle, with a

cap on it, so it would not stick him in his
pocket, put them on the sink, then, went in
his back pocket and pull out a small
comtainer, with some kind of substance in it,
that would not fill a eye droper, pour
(44)
it in the cap, as he was trying to get the last
drop out, the bus hit a hole in the road, it
jump off the sink on the floor, spilling what
ever he had left, he pull some toilet tissie off
the roll, trying to squeeze out what little he
had back in the cap, but that did not work,
the liquor narcotic was to small, he sit down
on the toilet, put his face in his hands.
 Saying dam to himself, that was the last fix
I had, until I get to L.A, putting his face
back
in his hands. A bright light from some where
shine on him, that was brighter than the rest
room light, he took his hands away from his
face, look up to see where it was coming
from, heard a voice saying, you are   mis-
treating my body, it is not to be use for
needles or puff of smoke, or srong drinks, I
only loan it to you for a little while to be on
this earth, to make good use of it, but if you
keep mis- useing it , I will return it back to
the dust, where it came from, remember, it is
not your body, the voice and light vanish,
with him sitting there in a daze, got up, put
his belt back in his pants, look in the mirrow
at himself,   his eyes was not delateing any
more, he smile, walking out of the rest-room,

without scratering. Lace got up to let him in to his seat, Tony still looking at him suspicion, like he did at his son, long time ago throught, man has put hell in this world for the young peoples, who are hook on that stuff, hopely it will come to a end, where man don,t have the knowledge to creat the wrong kind of meicine, that will not effect the body or its mind. Lace mutter out to the young man again, "Are you sure, that you don,t want to try my remedy?, In a soft voice saying "No thank you sir, I will be alright from now own", look out the window with a blance stare. Tony turn around, seening Gail and Tim, still sleeping, then back over to the young man, who eyes was not dilactng any more but still had that daze to them, with litlle tears coming out of the corner of his eyes, thinking of his son, and the young man, hoping that the Lord will brake the hold or monkey off their backs, he thought there is another one that had a experience, something in that rest-room, that is changing peoples back to the way, they are suppose to be. I hope it stay in there ,for everyone who coming on this bus, that is not right in what they are donig, it will make a whole new world, maybe I should have been on a bus, with a rest-room, like that in my young days. I have not been no angel myself, but I am trying, I gress that is all the Lord ask of us to try, life would be better for everyone, with our trials and tabulation also

our wrongs, we all might live to a right old age. Look back up front, met Queen Sheba eyes again, with her winking, as usual, he smile back, thinking, that sould of busrt her babble, laugh to himself, thinking, we are all most to L A, give the lady a brake, she turn around happy now. The Golden Girls was still sleep, so was Pat and lyn, the young men was talking to each other, Tony thought, they have got their friendship back together, before they get to L;A, he was getting ready to turn around to see what Tim and Gail was doing, but Tim pat him on the back saying, " What are you going to L.A for Pop,s? Tony mind went around to fine the right answer, to tell him, so he would not have to let out the real reason, for going utter, " I have relative out there, I have not seen in along time, thought, it was not a all lie, he had not seen his son in four years, answer, Tim, said "You are a long way from home", Tony reply back, " I know and will be glad to be heading back the other way, to my wife and kids", Tim qustion him again, " Was it that important for you to leave them and come this fare,Tony mind went seaching again for the right answer saying, " Yes Tim, one of them is sick and at the point of dead" which he was hoping and praying that these half lies, was not true, he did not want to tell him, that it was his son, he was about to brust opening from Tim
(45)

qustion, wishing he could tell him or someone the real deal of my two sons, the one twin son who is the hospital is the one he was talking about, he feld like a ballon about to bust open and hated to lie to his friends. Gail ask him, " Pop,s you look worry about

your relative? Tony said to her " I am Gail, I am, everything, will be all right when I get

there and see them, he turn back around, his mind clip back to his son, hoping Gail

and Tim undertood that lie, maybe in their minds, that I was going there for the real reaon, praying, saying to himself, not to much, longer to go, let me see him Lord, if you don,t do anything esle for me, let me see my son,s, with a smile on their faces and laughing together, me calling them in the house in the eveing of the day, Dwayne and Dwight, it is time to come in, before the sun hit your backs going down, everyone in the neigorhood could hear me calling them in before the sun went down, when they were boys, bring that joy back to them and me,.His mind was going around, like a whirl-pool, not stoping for any lights at all, the one in the hospital, only wanted to be love like every man from the opposite sex, not only pyhsical love, but the love of caring for each other, knowing each other in the right capacities, but at his age he pick the wrong kind of love and the wrong mate, like so many of us do when we are young or into our mature life, but what can we do, there is no signs on our backs to let who ever care fou you, saying I am the one, you just thrust in the Lord, hoping you have the right one, to make it through your exttinction, life is a close book, until you start flipping page atfer page of your life, past love and hurts, sometime that is not the answer, because this is a fast pace world, with no stoping of feeling for love, which is only seconardy to the pyhcisl love, which control our emoition within our bodys and mind, you can not go back to the past or fonward to the future, only stay were you are flipping a page a day in your life, maybe. I was born at the wrong time or I am in the wrong time or my thinking do not correlate with other peoples, but I do know there is happy-ness on them pages of life, we just have to find it, between the hurts and love, tiyng to give God a helping hand in this life.Tony thought started disapearing as his eyes close. The driver annonce we will be ariving in L.A in about   a   hour,   thank   you   for   riding Greyhound, I enjoy your company, you two young people in back, enjoy your marriage. Tony woke up look at Lace, saying, " You are almost home to see your wife and young ones,"Lace reply back, "Yes Pops as the kids in back of you call you, what is your name? "Well Lace we been riding a long time together, I am sorry that I did not induce myself, my name is Tony," then

Lace said "You know Tony, I miss them cowboys, Big Jack, Tiny and Phonco, all doe they talk about my life style, but they were fun." Tony reply back, "They were, if they were still on the bus, that preacher, will have to do a whole lot of hand waving in the air and praying ", the two of them laugh, then Tim but in," I miss them to, they taught me a lot of things about being a real man, when you have a mate, the responsibility, that go along with it and with a mate who love you."Tony and Lace agree with Tim., Tony eyes went in his fever pass time of looking up front , being noses again seen the Golden Girls, lyn,and Pat talking together, laughing, he could n,t hear that fare, so he just look out the window in the dark, because the sun had went down, thought, his nose all ways in people business, trying to hear what they are talking about, laugh to himself. One of the Golden Girl ask Pat and Lyn, where are you two staying at, while you are out here?, they said some hotel call the Hollywood Conformer, that the same one, where we will be at, we are going to have a lot of fun together, one of the other Golden girls utter, " I hope

(46)

they have a nice pool there, with plenty of young men, I have a blue bikini, that will knock their eye out, ". Lyn thorght I bet it will, when they see all them wringers over lapping each other ,Pat started patting on her wig , like it was real hair, saying I will just sit down in a pool chair, wearing my see though sumner dress and look, while they are looking back at me, knowing that I was a Hollywood star, Lyn thought again you are right about that, was, is the right word, I hope there is no wind out that day and they have sun glass on , because, if it blow off of her head, the sun bean down on it, they will not get blind from the rays bouneing off of that bold head, they will have a good surprise, laugh to herself, Pat look at her, knowing she was thinking something smart, but Lyn did,t say anything, just smile at her, like a kid, hiding a piece of canndy, Pat started back talking to another one of the Golden Girls, Lyn said to herself, what I got myself into, with all these old bags, trying to to be young again, I have another age on me instead of hanging out with these old hens, laugh again to herself.. The preacher was listening to them, put his hand back in the air, wavering it and praying Lord these mature ladie know that the age of their youth has by pass them, let them know they can,t go back their, let them konw they can only go forward, until you take hold their hands and take them home with you, then another thought jump into his head, saying they are kind of cute, and lovely to look at in their muture age, shook his head, saying get behind me devil, there no room in my world with God for that kind of thinking, then the devil pop up again," Is not you a man to ?, the preather, kelp on shaking his head, I said get away from me, fiinality his mind came to rest, with sweat coming off his forth head, from wrestling with the devil.. The driver pull up into L.A station, walk out to the luggeage carrier, started pulling out suitcases, everyone started getting their bags when they came out the laggage rack, the front started leaving off the bus first, Tony look at Queen Sheba leaving, she turn around and threw him a kiss, with her hand, Tony smile, did the same thing. Then the Golden Girls and Pat with Lyn, and the young men behind them. Tony and Lace, with Tim and Gail in back of them, everyone was out side now, getting their suit-cases, Tony pick his up and started toward the front door of the station, look to see only three cabs standing there, at the cab stand, he was getting ready to walk over to one when Tim and Gail came out the door, graping him around each side of his wist, saying, "We love you Pop,s, don,t forget to write when you get back to Dertoit", they were runing to get in the cab, Tony holler out, ! Hurried up and get home and start on a faimly," Tim holler back ! Yes, Pop,s yes," Gail just blush, and smile getting in the cab. Before he could get one of the other cab, the Golden Girls and Pat with Lyn came out the other doors and all of them took the last two cabs, while he was waiting for another cab to pull up at the cab stand, he look at his watch, setting on 10: P.M, said to himself, the hospital, advise us, we could come in at anytime. Then the two young men came out wailing together down the street, without the wiggle and inter a cab on the other side of the street, Tony thought, what ever was in that rest-room on the bus, did a good job, when they went in, while he was thinking, . Queen Sheba body guards pull up in her limousine and got out standing by it with that hard, look and no smile. He felt someone patting him on the back and turn around to see Queen Sheba as she put her arms around him kissing him on the lips, saying, " I been waiting three days on that bus to do that, I gress my hook was not big another to pull you in and laugh. " Tony kiss her back on her lips, utter, " Your hook was big enother, it just that someone else has all ready caught me on their hook, maybe

(47)

another time and age, we will ride another Grayhond together," I will miss winking at you bird-nest, with a tear at the corner of each eye and walk off to her limousine, while she was going, her body guards, who were at last smiling. Tony holler at her saying, ! I

will miss you to, with them pretty winking eyes and face, I never met anyone like you

before. " After they pull off, he hear a plane
up above and look up to see a bill broad sign
across the street saying The Queen of all
beauty supplys and cosmetics, with Queen
Sheba face on it, throught, why would she
be on a Grayhoud bus, insead of flying with
all that money, maybe she like being with
peoples, at the time he was thinking about
Queen Sheba, a cab pull up at the cab stand,
he went over to it and got in and said to the
driver St John hospital, the driver was
counting his fares, and said to himself, I
recognize that voice, he turn around saying,
" Is that you Dad," he had a small beard on
his face, Tony didn,t recognize him at first,
utter, " Is that you Dwayne," the two of
them, jump out the cab and run around to
each other,with tears in their eyes, and grap
each other Dwayne said " Why are you here
Dad," Tony reply, " You didnt know that
your brother Dwight was in the hospital at
the point of dead from H.I.V? Dwayne drop
to his knees on the side walk, Tony pull him
up and he said, " I and Dwight broke up
long time ago, because he was associating
with the wrong kind of people, like me in
my young days, with that narcotic habit, I
put you and mom, though hell with myself,
please forgive me dad and tell mom to
forgive me to when you get back, I kick the
habit a year ago and don,t be around
peoples that is on it, they will find out if you
don,t let it go, a grave is waiting for you, I

myself like to be in this world a little longer. " The two drove off to the hospital, with silence between each other, as they pull into the hospital parking lot, got out, not knowing what to expeck when they got to Dwight room, walk through its door,, still not saying anything to each other. They walk up to the reception desk, Tony ask could you pleae tell us which way is I.C.U, to see my son, Dwight Albert, they were direct to it. The two walk away to I.C.U , pluse at the door, like they were afraid to go in, Tony may the first move, walk though them,with Dwayne behind him into I.C.U, and seen Dwight there laying in a hospital bed, looking pale, intravenous needle in each arm and a heart monitor by him, with Tony looking at it, the images of a mountain range going back and forward, Tony kept looking at it hoping it, stay like that, they walk over to his bed, as Dwayne pull a chiar up on the other side of the bed, took his hand into his, holding it, Tony pull a chair up to his ear so he could whisper the affirmation of the lord and strength, with his mind to him, said to Dwight, say these word every second and every minute and hour of the day and night, keep repeating them, son. " I am a child of God and my body and mind is working in proper normal order and my cells are renew and realizing there selfs, beinging more energy and electric to my body at all time ", son keep

repeating it over and over. Dwight eye lips
was trying to open all while Tony was
talking to him, Tony kelp looking at Dwight
heart monitor all the time he was talking,
than the moitor went into a straight line,
meaning Dwight heart had stop, Tony push
the panic button on the bed, the nurses
came running with a heart reaiizer, saying to
us, " Stand back," while they work on
Dwight, they hit him three time in the chest,
with no effect from each shock, one of the
nurses said to, Tony, " I am sorry Mr, we
could not bring him back" with sad eyes,
He is in the hands of the Lord now. " Tony
look at her with tears in his eyes, said
slowely, " What will be, will be " all of the
nurses walk out the room, with the
machine..Tears came out of his eyes, saying
to himself, thank you Lord,
 (48)
for letting me get here for what little time I
had with him, still thinking about what he
said to the nurse and that he should of
apologie to her for telling her the reality of
dead and life, so cold,, but all of us can,t live
in a make belive world ,we can,t by pass
this in

                         Chapter 10
life, what going to be will be and face up to
the real world, for we loose the ones we love
in dead and in this life, we can,t morn the
ones that leave us in dead or our lifes,

because life is to short, to take all your time with who, have left you behind, you must face the reatily of it, but it hurt, because you are only inside a humen body, were there is feeling and emoition to go along with it. Than he felt on his knees and cry out ! God why, please why,don,t take any more of my kids, take me and let them have more of life in this beautiful world of yours, Dwayne drop own on his knees, beside him, and put his arms around his shoulders, was crying to, he look at Dwayne, who was still holding his hand, hollering ! Come back Dwight, come back. " Tony remember his repeated dream on the bus, with Dwayne trying to pull Dwight out the river from drowning and I holding his hand, but Dwight hand slide away from Dwayne hand and I pull him to safety, now he knew what that dream was about, Dwight leaving us and Dwayne staying. Dwayne was still holding on to Dwight hand, said to Tony," His hand is getting cold "Dad," with tears rolling down on his face, Tony, utter, " I know son, he is know longer in that body, he has went home where there is only peace and love. " They walk out of I.C.U after the Doctor had pronounce, Dwight decease, walk down the hall, with their arms around each other shoulders, went through the doors of the hospital, back to the cab, Tony was getting in, , said to Dwayne, " Is there a beach around here?, he, answer, "Yes, Santa

Momcia beach, why do you want to go there? Tony reply I just want to rest my mind and body saying, " that is the same place were Dwight was staying in a apartment, at, by the content in his bill fold that I took out of his hospital draw ", Dwayne muse, " let me see Dad " and Tony handed him the paper with the address on it , Dwayne utter, " You right Dad, we will be passing by there on the way to the beach, do you want to stop? Tony reply " No, you can drop me off there on the way back". They pull up at the beach, park, Tony got out and pull his shoses, with his socks off, through them back in the cab, as Dwayne did the same thing, the two walk down to the beach bare footed not saying a word, sit down in the sand, rolling there pants up so they would not get wet from the waves coming in, with a full moon above shining on the water, it was a pretty sight, Tony thought, and look at the waves coming in pulling some of the grains of sand back down to the botten and being some back up with it. and said to Dwayne, " You know them wave are just like life, taking life back to the dust, as the waves take grains of sand back to the bottem and being it back up as a woman wound being life back in the world to replace the one who went back to the dust, we came from the dust and we must go back, the choice is yours to make your life short or long in what ever you do in this life, it is a cycle,, one go and one come back, it like the waves and sand, some go back with the replacement, of others, the molder of your life is God and you, for you to make it right or wrong and we are the ones, with the make up kit, to being joy to ourselfs, our mate or who ever we are associate with. We only have a short time in this world, bcause years are like miinutes in this life.You have to love yourself in order to love someone else and do what ever your destiny call for.. You can,t down the other peson for their forks or judge their life style,

 (49)

no matter what color they are, or trying to be what they want to be, we all is the same, just our ways of living and thinking is what change a person,, this is the same as a mate, it is not their ways of life or yours, but the thinking of each other, this is the confusing of the two with the world of people coming in, unilil they find each other way of thinking about life and relationship, butmaintain our own, and leave a legacy of good behind, if it is only love and noning else, love is the key word to happy-ness, without it you are lose. Dwayne utter back, " You know Dad, you are right if you don,t love yourself and be happy, you can,t love someone else and make them happy.". The two went silent, just look up at the full moon and then at the waves banging sand up from the bottom, taking it back down, like life leaving and coming back, to the world, as sand come into the shore, like life starting all over again and then back to the dust.

GRAYHOUND

THE END.

Auther: Wilson Albert Jr.(Tony Wilson, Musician name)

Forward

Rising children and helping mold themselfs
into the right person, for this society and the
rest of their extinction, in this world of trails
and tribulation, so hurn can,t come to them while
they are traveling though their years. The Lord
and you are the molders of their destiny
though their adolescent, to be the right man or
woman. You can,t be the big bad wolfe and
chastise for every little thing or a lamb and over

look the thing they do, you have to show love in each situation in order to maintain your postion.

As a father or a mother. This is only my veiw, on rising children, by rising six of them

Content

This book, is about the struggle of a faimly man survival, in this world to keep his faimly together and trying to keep the grips of the world hibits away from his twin sons but they were still intice into its net work. He had to leave Deroit, Mi, and ride a Greyhound bus, for three days, to Los Angeles, California. He met people who was traveling to the West Coast also and became their friends, telling each other their problens, acept him, because of his pride.

Acknowlegment

This book has no reflection on Greyhound or its drivers it was writen in 1991, after he had exprie before the tranportion laws was change to no smoking on any tranportion, while traveling. There is no reflection, with its plots on any group or person, all charters and plots, are fictitouis, acept for I and my twin sons, which is a true story.

Dedication
This book is dedicated, to my twin sons Dwayne and Dwight

Albert also my wife, Linda J Albert.
Dwight expire in 1991, my wife
expire in 2006, of cancer, Dwayne is
still missing. That leave three young
ladies , Lillie Albert, zawadi
Albert,Tamika Albert and Wilon
Albert lll the oldest son. The next
Generation are my three wonderful
adopted children Antoine Albert,
Elleia Albert, and Latasha Albert
which make up the rest of the clan
and took the place of the ones that we
lost. like I say in the book theres
always some kind of way to replace
whatever, you lost through life or
death So I say to you, all readers of
this book may God
Bless you. I hope that this book may
put some incite on your feeling of
losing someone through heartbrake or
them passing on to be with the Lord.

(1)   **The**
Block

One block out of the city streets, are
line with yellow and red brick ranch
  type homes, with bay windows and
green shrublerys around each one and
  niceley cut green lawns, looking like
any other city block, but Burt Rd is
  not, because of the un-usual things
that happen on that block. The
  residences of that block are some
young people and mostely elderly
ones
  with about ten kids in all, there was a
old time Marine in his 80's who sit
  on his front proch, before day brake,
every day, with a camouflage cap on
  and a red Marine Corp pull over
sweater, with blue jean and tennis
shoes
  taking in with his eyes, like he was
still in the Marines, what he could see
that time of moring, looking around
like he was on, petrol in the service,
his house was the only one on the
block, with black rail and a black
panther
 statue by the steps, with green eyes,
that would, scare anyone in the dark,
by

the handicap ram because he had a handicap daughter of twenty-five, who   could not walk or talk, she was born with Cerebral Palsy, but she is smarter than the ones, who don,t have any infliction of their bodys.Her mind is
 functioning in the right capacity, because with that one hand that she use,
 can make communication for what she want and don,t want, with a finger
 sign and everyone knows what that mean. By using that finger justice, you
 tell evrything that she needs, but you have to be around her all the time to
 know what she is coversing to you. Latashe, has been in the Albert family,
 sent she was born, with two other adopted kids. And six of his own.
 Everyone has departed him to live their lifes, accept for one of his son
 and a grandson, with one daughter, who help with Latasha,
 . Mr Albert, wife pass away ten year,s ago, leaving him with Latasha
 making him a father and a mother. Mr Albert, the man with two first

names, Wilson Albert, watching the
street, up and down, seeing the new
paper delivery man and helper, a big
dog coming down the street, with the
 dog on a long leases, running beside
the car, with a new paper in it mouth,
 slanging it to each house, as the man
in the car, pass the papers and he
would slang it where ever it land, on
the sidewalk or lawn, sometime, it
make it to there porch. Mr Albert
thought to himself, I be dam, that dog
has a job and all these young people
can,t find one, or not paying enough
for   their taste. The back yard
of the houses, mostly had private
fences around
them, like Mr Albert, but his was
open in back of the garage, were he

 (2)
could see into the lady next door to
him yard, who was of African desent,
she worn white long African attire all
the time like she was a vigil, at that

age, he would wonder, and a white
gele wrap around her head and
differrent
 kind of color beads around her neck
and bare feet, with them feet, she
could
 step on anything and it would not
hurn, them, Mr Albert throught, and
watching her from the side of his
garage,and the chickens marching
around,   she did not see him, still
thinking about her feet. Peeking at
her, pulling weeds out her garden and
not turning, until she hear her
chickens making noise and seen Mr
Albert, with a childist smile on his
face, being noises
 about her business, the garden was
by a fence, of the chicken coop
  with five chicken in it, lookimg at
her as she was singing and pulling
  weeds up, and started marching
around in the coop to the sound of
voice, like they where troops in a
parade review, for the higher up, on a
service parade ground , waiting for
Top Sergeant to get thru, with her
work.

She also had a whistle around the beads, and braids, he thought any other person, with have a dog for a pet, but she has chichen and he kept thinking, why she keep that whistle around her neck and what do she do with it? The next day he went back around the side of of the garage to clean up and found out why she had that whistle around her neck and laugh to himself, when he seen her blowing it, lining up the chicken in mitaery form, he was still laughing at her in silent, so she would would not hear him and thinking that lady, is off her rocker, as she turn and met his eyes, shining and wide open, with a guilty look on his face, as he smile again, with a little grim, saying, "Do you want sell, one of those big fat hens, I need one for my dinner, and being you a plate, if you want one, they look good to eat", her eyes roll around in her head and she holler,! Are you insane, you want to eat one of my babys, take your old self back in the house and cook your own food, if you are hnugey and don,t

think about eating my chickens.with
that big noses eyes of yours. Still
 smiling, he look at her and mutter, "
Well, I just ask, sent you had so many,
 one out the rant, would,nt hurt your
line up, Mrs Sheba," she roll her eyes
at him, hollering again, ! Dont you
have something better to do with your
old butt, or a wife or anyone else to
irridate their day, beside me, and quit
calling, me Mrs Sheba and put a
handle on my name, it is Queen Sheb
and buy you a pet to keep you
company, and quit calling me Mrs
Sheba."
 He walked away toward his back
proch, with a smile on his face,
thinking

 (3)
 how she call me an old man, she is no
spring chicken herself, as he was
allmost to his porch, she holler again, !
And don,t open that car trumk of
yours, that you call a mouth. He just
shook his head, saying to himself,

that lady, need a over hule on her mind, she must have been a drill instrctor
in the Corp, the way she have them chicken train to walk in a line, and sit
down on his back prock, and looked up, saying Lord help her and them chicken. About 1:00 A:M in the moring, Queen Sheba was woke up wi th
her chickens, making a lot of nose, she jump up runing to her back door,
with her shot gun in her hand and tip outside, seeing a man with all back on to bind in with the night, with two of her chickens in each hand, as he was trying to get over the back fent, she took aid and shot him in the butt,
he drop the chickens and grap his butt, which was full of beck shots and
and his pants, that have feld down off of his butt and went over the fent.
Mr Albert, wsa woke up with all the nose outside and went out the back to
see what was happening and seen Queen Sheba out by her back fent, talking to her chickens. " That old bad man, try to take my babys, but I fix

him, it will be a long time before he can sit down again," and blew her wistle, as the two chickens line up and walk back into their coop and she walked back into her house. Mr Albert just shook his head and looked up again, not thinking about her. The next moring, he was sitting on his frout

he seen a police stco car pull up in front of her house and stop, talking he thought, look like Mrs Queen Sheba is in trobule, about last night

Queen Sheba seen them to and sarted blowing her wisthle, lining her chicken up, marching them thoungh the side door, down into the basment, as they march, popbin there heads with each step, like some one was calling

Marine Corp kadining. The police got out of their car and went knocking on her side gate, as she opening it, with I am insent smile on her face, as she muse, " Can I help you offices," yes, the niegors said they hear gun stots over in your back yard last night and you had chicken back there, looking sucsoue at her, and said can we come in and look around, her eyes look up and then down at the officers and utter in a slofe voice, " come on in, I have noning to hide, them neigors, have me mix up with another house. They walked in the yard and seen the fent in chicken coop and ask her what was that for, she look at them and than up again, knowing she was getting read to tell a lie, saying, that was my dog house, he pass away and I never torn it down, one of the officer said he must have been a big dog, she reply, "Yes he was, a big pit bull," thay just looked at her and walk out the gate to their car, as they were headed to their car, one of them ask the ofter one laughing, " Did you see her feet," his partner bust out laughing, getting in the car utter I would hate to have them rubing up agaisnt mind in bed and laugh until tears was coming out of his eyes.

Printed in Poland
by Amazon Fulfillment
Poland Sp. z o.o., Wrocław